HOUSTON IN SEPTEMBER

by S.E. Saunders

Cover photo from stock photos on pexels.com

Edited by Mandi Summit, Red Quill Co LLC

Cover design by Beth Holtz

Author's Note

Thank you for reading *Houston in September.* While I list the publication as book nine of the A Year in Romance series, this book is the first written in the series.

Each book is a standalone story. The theme is tied together by the months of a year. You do not need to read any of the other books in the series to understand this book.

Acknowledgments

To Kelly. For saying, "I can see you sitting over there, signing your books." When we stood in the bookstore. For taking a chance on me, when I was a single mother, for your love, devotion and care. I told you I didn't do an acknowledgement… and I didn't, not for the author copy. I made sure I did it for the proper, going out to everyone else who happens to read my book copy. Yes, I'm crying.

To Nathan, Beth, and Pina this book will be here long after I'm gone. I hope when you read it you'll think of me and laugh at the parts that made me laugh. I love you so very much. Be good. Do good.

For Mandi Summit, Editor and a phenomenal writer in her own right. Without your professionalism, guidance, encouragement, and suggestions I am fairly sure this book wouldn't have seen the light of day. Thank you.

Welcome to Texas

Emilia Patric removed her rose-rimmed reading glasses and flung them carelessly onto the fold-out tray in front of her, mildly shocked at the clatter as their frame struck the cheap plastic. *What a steaming pant load. Handshake business deals? Stubbornly sticking to one product line? The man has zero business sense.* With a hand at her neck, she massaged the knot of tension that had accumulated during the five-hour flight.

In the same row two chairs to her right, a triangular-faced man with dark brown hair and hazel eyes jolted awake. His movement shaking the row of seats they shared.

"You're staring. Aren't you? How much longer?" he said from under his sleep mask.

Emilia considered not answering, but Danny had an uncanny knack for knowing when her eyes were on him even when he slept.

"Thirty minutes or so."

"What's wrong?"

"Well, aside from looking at your hideous mask with eyeballs and lashes for the last five hours. I need a vacation." She shut the lid of her laptop. "I have zero figs to give. I'm two milliseconds away from sending off an email to the chief executive officer of Hex Holdings to ask if he purchased his MBA for twenty-nine, ninety-five."

"You do realize the saying is f—?" Danny halted mid-sentence. "What? Ms. Neurotic needs a vacay? Hold me, Mrs. Patric. I must be dreaming." He sat up and repositioned himself, pulling his sleep mask up to his forehead to stare deeply into her smoke-colored, gold-flecked eyes.

"Oh, zip it, you dunderhead. You know why."

"Sorry, Emmi. It's a good idea. I'll handle the meat and potatoes of 'meeting-land.' You can tan your tootsies or tweak your tassels in Galveston. Lord knows you haven't taken any time to…" Letting the sentence fade purposefully, he rawred and then steepled his fingers, a look of pure devilry stealing across his pointy face.

"You look like the love child of Ace Frehley and Tim Curry when you do that. Stop it." She raised a hand to palm his face across the seat. "Don't even think it, Danny Davinski. I'm not going out to find a man."

"You're no fun at all, Emmi the neurotic elephant."

"Nor am I packing my trunk and saying goodbye to my circus." She laughed, thinking of how they'd met twenty years ago at a punk concert.

Danny, ever the non-conformist, stood outside the washroom listening to her retch during a particularly nasty bout of the stomach flu.

"Man, I've only heard people doing that on cassette tape," he remarked nonchalantly through the stall door.

"I'm in here doing it live. Not enjoying it," she replied weakly as she held the toilet bowl.

"Do, you need me to hold your hair or anything?"

"No, but it's kind of you to offer." Fifteen-year-old Emilia came out to rinse her mouth only to meet the skinniest kid with a two-foot-tall black mohawk. While their paths had gone separate ways, they'd recently rekindled their friendship after Danny applied to an advert she posted for a personal assistant shortly after Mason's death and launching her new business.

Returning her thoughts to the present, Emmi said, "Thanks for the reminder though—it's been a while since I took in a punk concert."

"There's the spirit. Call me when you reach the hotel. I'm sorting out details with the crew and pilot."

"No hitting on the pilot. Capiche?"

"It's not as if they haven't already asked for my number." He winked, rubbing his hands together deviously.

"Reprobate."

Forty-five minutes later, Emilia stepped into Houston's heady heat. A frown appeared on her face as she smoothed wrinkles from her white dress and stared at the wall of passengers in front of her. She propped a hand over her brow and scanned the crowd for where the bottleneck originated. *I knew it.* As expected, her gaze landed on a group of garishly dressed women chatting in the middle of the walkway.

Emilia weaved her way down the plane stairs, her mule shoes echoing on the metal. Her lips drew into a thin grim line, as she headed toward the cluster. "Ladies, please keep the line moving. There are still several passengers yet to deplane."

"Who the hell does she think she is?" asked one of the women who was busy applying lipstick in a compact mirror as Emilia walked away.

"Some Karen. No doubt under the assumption she can police everyone's behavior."

Overhearing the exchange, Danny approached them, his Oxfords tapping out a clipped staccato upon the tarmac. His good looks commanding the attention of all the women present. "Mrs. Patric, please wait," he called above the women's gossip.

Emmi pivoted on her red sole to face him. "Yes?"

"You forgot your scarf." Danny passed it almost reverently into her hand.

Emmi stared at the expensive silk twill and felt the fabric's hand-rolled edges wistfully. The stag and forest creature motif a reminder to accept the luxuriant experiences nature offered—one of the last gifts Mason had given her.

"Thank you, Danny." She retied the scarf at her neck, one foot already turning back to her intended direction, eager to be out of the direct sun.

Seeing his boss wielding carry-on luggage, laptop bag, and purse, Danny called after her, "Are you certain you don't want me to call a porter?"

"Not necessary," Emilia fired back. With a dismissive wave, she plodded off.

"We'll take the cart," one of the loitering women stated, a conspiratorial smile creeping across her countenance.

Danny dialed up a chilly gaze for the woman as he assessed her and her companion's cheetah-print-clad forms. "Terribly sorry. The service is reserved for VIPs and the infirm."

"Then why did you offer her one? Is she infirm?" one of the women sniggered, shooting a death glare of jealousy at Emilia's departing figure.

"No. She's the Karen who chartered the plane to the tune of ten thousand dollars per hour. Get your attention-seeking, fake-tanned tocks moving. Now," he barked in a tone not far removed from that of a drill sergeant.

With above average hearing, Emilia exchanged a satisfied look with him, then dropped a sleek pair of sunglasses over her eyes. Breaking with the niceties of social protocol, she swept forward, leaving the scent of citrus and fresh blooms in her wake.

Welcome to Texas.

Entering the airport, the AC floundered under the crush of people. Kiosks and quirky food venues thronged with life. Impatient customers stood ten deep as they waited to get their mitts on items more edible than the packet of pretzels presented during the flight. The smell of freshly ground coffee permeated the air. Staff crisscrossed in imaginary lanes wearing professionally pinched faces as reuniting families hugged in joy, while others unknowingly embraced in bittersweet forever goodbyes.

Emmi's heart constricted, watching as a soldier clad in uniform covered his wife's face with welcome kisses. *Why did you come?* mocked her injured heart. *Mrs. Patric, we regret to inform you…* Emmi squeezed her eyes closed, pushing the memory away.

Cell in hand, she found a position out of the way of foot traffic, taking a moment to compose herself before searching her bag for the hotel email she had printed. *Of course, it's at the blooming bottom*, she thought as she rifled below everything else piled on top of it.

"Hello, this is Mrs. Patric… George Bush International… Mhm… Yes… A5? Thank you, I'll be waiting."

Finished with the call, she lined up alongside the baggage carousel waiting for several rotations until the bright yellow tag of her case came into view. Grabbing it, she pointed the wheels toward the ground, extended the handle, and lit off, escaping the area before subsequent aircraft unloaded passengers.

Strazzo Eton's taxi pulled up to the George Bush International extremely late having passed through heavy rush hour traffic.

He reached forward to tip the driver from the back seat. "Keep the change," he instructed. Strazzo didn't pause long enough to witness the operator's response to the generous sum on top of his regular fare. It always made him feel awkward.

The lid of the trunk popped open as he approached. Grabbing his carry-on, he hoisted its wide black strap over his head and settled it between neck and shoulder. Slamming the lid shut, he thumped the back of the vehicle to let the driver know he'd finished and rushed at the airport doors.

On cue, the sleek blue watch on his left wrist flashed with an urgent reminder of flight departure. Lengthening his stride, he sidestepped dawdling passengers on their way through the automatic opening to stand at the nearest ticket wicket. Tapping through the prompts with expertise, he grabbed the ticket as it fell. *Customs better not be the equivalent of a parking lot on Black*

Friday, he thought. Readjusting his ball cap to partially block his face, he jogged the short distance and positioned himself in the express check-in line.

A crowd of approximately fifty people stood opposite him ignoring his presence as they conversed with their loved ones or tended to business on their devices. The surrounding noise produced a quiet hum. Relieved he had gone unnoticed thus far, he glanced around until a loud phony cough shattered the relative quiet.

"Isn't that…?" A short, ginger-haired woman with unruly curls pointed, grabbing her friend's jacket frantically. Her unevenly penciled-in eyebrows wiggled animatedly as she tried to quell the squeal from her lips.

"Houston's Finest?" The friend tittered as she made eyes his way, waving her sausage-sized fingers at him—Strazzo Eton, Hex Holdings hottie, as the regional media dubbed him.

They're like a bad car accident, he thought as he eyed the pair. His distaste fleeting in the minutest micro expression.

The friend wore two-sizes-too-small black yoga leggings, a chunky top, and dirty sneakers.

She appeared dwarfish, but not in terms of height. Rather, she was as wide as she was tall. Although he liked his women curvaceous, he suspected if he looked close enough this one was bearded.

Worse, she hadn't shut up in the ten minutes he'd been standing there, and on his father's grave, if he heard the snap of her gum one more time, he was going to shove it down her throat. He was accustomed to dealing with fanatical slobs who imagined they'd catch his attention, but these women weren't simply sorely mistaken, they were downright delusional.

Strazzo compared them to the models he had dated in the last year. A buxom blonde, a catty brunette, the sporty redhead with a set of stems that haunted his dreams. He wasn't much for ink, but he traced the arms of her octopus tattoo down her abdomen with the enthusiasm of a boy on his first bicycle.

He'd also wiled away time pursuing a prominent heiress. Although he regarded her as a tree-hugging hippy, her ability to turn him down multiple times presented the type of challenge he never got tired of showing up to. Even she had better style than these two duds put together. Still, his admirers had certain expectations of his rich playboy persona.

He stripped off his sports jacket deliberately. Maintaining seductive eye contact, he loosened the top button of his collar. His fingertips worked the Kelvin knot of his tie as he eyed the women, smiling as their mouths fell open over his seemingly sensual undress. The taller of the two fanned herself wildly to stop from hyperventilating.

"Damn, girl," he cooed like an adoring lover, expertly playing the part expected of him. He sidled past their position through the check-in. With a wink and a smile, he was out of their reach and off to customs. *Booyah, ugly britches.*

Running through the airport toward his gate, his gaze homed in on a curvy brunette in a white dress. He had to do a double take to be sure it wasn't his wing woman. *Nah,* he reminded himself. *Sondra isn't due in until after my plane departs.* Strazzo looked away, trying to forget how disappointed he was to miss her by mere minutes.

***

Two months prior…

"While buying your mom a family ring dripping with emeralds, you can stick this on your credit card also. With love, from you to me." Sondra's dark eyes flashed with humor as she modeled an exquisite ring with sassy flair. "Be a love, would you? Get down on one knee and present this to me."

"Why would I do that?" he snapped defensively, avoiding her eye contact. Grabbing the ring, he returned the eighteen-karat gold and platinum, diamond-studded monstrosity to the jeweler.

Sondra rolled her eyes and tilted her chin with an air of faux haughtiness. "Anyone forced to deal with your annoying antics deserves it. That, or a handwritten induction into the hall of patron saints."

"Saint Sondra, patron saint of Strazzo. Now, that *would be nuts." He grinned, holding the door to the shop open for her. "Get outta here."*

***

Strazzo had laughed it off in the moment, but shortly after, he'd found himself compelled to return to the store following the siren call of the ring and all the possibilities that came along with it. Two months had passed since then as he deliberated the right time to spring it on her, or if he even could at all.

Sondra had been that person who was always there for him through thick and thin—and Strazzo definitely got into the thick of it from time to time. Ever loyal, Sondra was his best friend. But something about that day in the jewelry store opened his eyes to the possibility of something more.

As he pondered his underlying reluctance to give the bobble to Sondra, in his nearby periphery the brunette in the white dress narrowly evaded the hard-shelled luggage trailing behind a businesswoman. White Dress Woman pitched forward as her baggage zipped in one direction and her foot slid in yet another.

He rushed to her position, threw off the coat he carried, and reached for her. Instead of steadying the woman as envisioned, his open hand smacked against the round rise of the woman's taut buttocks. The sound ricocheted loud enough to draw curious stares in their direction, and pink to his cheeks.

Humiliated and concerned over the potential of another lawsuit, Strazzo raised his hands, removing them from the vicinity of the woman's derrière. His best intention a straight road to hell as his cuff raked the rough edge of the woman's cotton dress, snagged the front of the bodice, and tore the fabric away. Shocked to see the woman's breasts, Strazzo stared. Then panicked. Raising his hands instinctively to cover her chest. His chivalry backfired when she indignantly delivered a crisp, resounding slap across his face.

"Get your damn hands off of me!" White Dress Woman hissed, hastily tucking her breasts back inside the tattered bodice.

"*Perdonami, per favore. Ho sbagliato.*" Strazzo stumbled off an apology in Italian, unconsciously reverting to his mother tongue, mortified that he had palmed the perky peaks of a stranger.

Her face contorted as she continued to readjust her dress. Pushing against his chest, she felt her foot sliding out again on the over-polished tile. She gasped as she folded inward, her most intimate parts grinding against the hard muscle of the man's upper thigh.

Holding her upright, Strazzo felt every microscopic inch of the woman crushed against him. Smelling the light scent of her perfume and feeling the silken slide of her glossy brown hair, he groaned inwardly. Not daring to shift out of the cringe-worthy position, afraid fate conspired to concoct another folly, he froze every muscle and waited for her to tell him exactly what to do.

"Maybe if you lift?" she suggested as she clung to his waist tenuously.

Averting his eyes from the juncture of the woman's thighs, he lifted her, struggling not to notice as White Dress Woman's hem rode up to reveal even more.

Emilia noticed his purposefully averted gaze and, glancing down, realized what he was avoiding. She quickly tugged at her hem, regaining her privacy, but losing her composure. Face flushed, she glanced at the mid-twenties man who both saved and humiliated her in a single act. His face contrasted cherubic charm with a definitive aura of cocky superiority. Rounding out his looks were lively, intelligent eyes which stared into hers uncomfortably.

"*Grazie.*" Emmi said brusquely as she leaned in to retrieve the man's passport and coat from the floor, before handing them off.

"*Guarda dove vai, piccolo ghepardo,*" Strazzo said, testing her knowledge of the language. *Watch where you are going, little cheetah.* He took his items, wondering about the chances of a tryst.

"Now boarding flight 0119 to Paris," an automated voice blared from the loudspeaker.

Strazzo started, realizing he'd tarried much longer than intended.

"Thank you for saving me from what promised to be a disastrous fall. I'm staying at Post Oak. Emilia Patric." She stuck out her hand to shake his in a professional manner. "Maybe I could treat you to a beverage?"

Misinterpreting the friendly offer, Strazzo held onto Emilia's hand and examined her under a fringe of dark lashes, amazed at the similarities between herself and Sondra. *She has a beautiful face. Banging body.* He let go of her hand and glanced away briefly before returning eye contact. *Still, she's no Sondra.*

"Sorry, I can't," he said with a tinge of regret. "They've announced my flight."

"Then, I guess this is goodbye…" Emilia stated, hoping the inflection of her voice would elicit the man's name

"Dante Alighieri," he introduced swiftly, having a bit of fun. Surely, this woman knew who Strazzo Eton, millionaire playboy was?

Emmi frowned, eyebrows furrowing into a pinched V, her eyes narrowing like she'd seen a slithering thing deserving of a beating. "Your name is Dante Alighieri?" she said slowly, allowing him time to correct his lie.

"Yes," Strazzo replied straight-faced, trying his best to sound earnest. He was amused at the fact that this enigmatic creature didn't know him, nor his well-deserved reputation.

"You're a damned liar and as likely to be named Dante Alighieri as Dante's life work is to be translated true to the Latin it's penned in. Don't bother looking me up, I don't drink with d-bags."

"Hoo." Strazzo wolf-whistled as she strode off, chuckling when she flipped him the bird with a red-tipped, stiletto nail.

Reaching the taxi queue, Emilia strolled the length of the raised concrete pad, rubbernecking for her ride. *That's a first*, she thought, impressed to find the vehicle parked exactly where the hotel administrator said it would be. At her approach, a well-kempt long-haired driver with a wide, friendly smile, popped from the van. "Everything okay, Miss Perric?" He drawled in an unexpected yet hoped for Texan accent, offering his hand in a grip of a steady handshake.

"Fine," she replied curtly, not noticing the mistake in last name through his thick accent. She was still annoyed about the exchange between herself and Not-Dante. *Shake it off. It's not like you'll see that fool again.*

"Let me get your things." The driver grabbed her suitcase. While waiting, she drew the oversized laptop bag off her shoulder. "Appears you're traveling light. What brings you to the Lone Star State?"

"Business," she remarked, her thoughts shifting to her itinerary. Unwilling to get into the discussion that would surely follow, she left out the details. Her firm was breaking ground on a multiplex devoted to the North American Military Widows Support Foundation.

Her passion project had come into existence during her first year as a widow. She remembered all too clearly how she had tried to navigate death benefits, support groups, and coming to terms with being a widow at much too young an age, thinking how fortunately unfortunate she was that she and Mason didn't have children. With barely enough headspace for herself, she had stifled her grief and turned her career into therapy.

After earning her first billion in the semiconductor industry, the idea of building a foundation from the ground up to help bereaved widows and widowers navigate the system seemed less daunting. Although the name suggested only military widows would benefit, the services provided would offer numerous programs for civilians as well.

Hearing the words *accent* and *from* above the sharp echo of blaring horns as the driver continued to make small talk, she remarked, "Originally, Canada."

"Always wanted to go there. What part of the country?" he continued in a swift interrogative fashion.

"West—"

"Excuse me," a curly-haired woman interrupted, breezing past Emilia to speak directly to the shuttle driver, a considerable amount of luggage trailing behind her. "I'm certain this is my shuttle."

Emilia withdrew to the side of the van, not taking much notice of the woman. She politely ignored the bulk of the conversation between them until the woman's voice took on an irate tone. "I'll be calling the Eton's about this." The woman pivoted on her heel and hurried off in a huff.

"Sorry," the driver apologized, the shine of his accommodating self momentarily tarnished. He eyed Emilia for a moment as if searching for something. Shaking his head slightly, he slid into the driver's seat and fastened his seatbelt.

"Careful with that word. Soon, you'll be mistaken for Canadian," Emilia ribbed him gently.

With the smile restored to the driver's face, Emmi withdrew the magazine she'd purchased earlier and fanned herself, grateful for the blast of cool air that ripped through the van.

"Hold on," he instructed. Throwing the vehicle into gear, the van zipped from behind the line of numerous automobiles in the packed pickup zone. Scant minutes later, they peeled out of the airport lot, exited onto a business frontage road, and sped up to jockey for position on the frenetic freeway. The driver executed a feat Emilia thought would take fifteen minutes at the very least in only six.

But twenty minutes later, her confidence in the driver waned as the van careened off to a side road and veered onto a quieter residential street.

"We're in the wrong neighborhood. We've entered The Woodlands," Emilia asserted. She tapped the map on her phone as they whizzed by single-family residences. "We should be over by The Galleria."

"I know where I'm going," The driver responded peevishly.

Shocked at the shift in the way he spoke to her, Emmi felt the hairs stand up on her neck as her mind raced to make sense of what was happening. The driver proceeded to ignore her until they pulled through the black wrought iron gates of a painstakingly landscaped mansion.

"We've arrived," he said without looking at her.

Emmi's heart leaped in her chest, eyes wide as she stared at the stocky men patrolling the grounds. *How are you this naïve? This looks like one of those hussy houses. Come on, Canadian bacon. Figure a way out of this.*

Emmi's gaze darted to the driver once more, now certain she was about to be a victim of ransom or trafficking. Discreetly, she slipped her shoes from her feet and grabbed the door handle. Inching it open, she prayed the crunch of tires on gravel would stifle the sound of it sliding on its rail.

"What the hell?" The driver stared in shock as his passenger ditched the van and rolled out onto the grass. His expression priceless as she hiked her skirt and tore off across the expanse of the grounds.

At her sudden movement, a couple of soot-snouted, black and tan German shepherds bayed with enthusiasm. Their lean shapes set off after her as they defiantly disregarded their master's clipped commands.

Lithe legs driving under her, she shrieked, "Nice puppies!" Her fleet feet carried her terrified five-foot-five frame across the lawn as the furred missiles with snarling lips and gnashing teeth homed in on her position.

Tossing her nine-hundred-dollar shoes into the air, she zig-zagged in the opposite direction, bum cheeks bouncing and visible to all as she ran past everyone like a marathoning, half-nude streak. Blessedly, the hounds stopped to sniff and gnaw her leather footwear. She slunk past them, heart hammering against her ribs from the steady exertion.

Fixing her gaze upon the wrought iron surrounding the grounds, she barreled down on the shorter of the two men who stood there. *What had her self-defense instructor said? Hard palm. Go for the shaded areas. Twist and pluck his peaches.*

The poised guard inclined his ear toward the radio attached to his shoulder as it chirped.

His eyes locked on Emilia's advancing form as he listened to the instructions.

Time to pluck some peaches.

"Please advise Sondra after her run that she cuts a fine figure of a runner. I'm quite impressed by her performance."

Catching a smattering of the guard's conversation, Emilia slowed and looked toward the raised concrete balustrade of the manse. A wide-shouldered man stood at the railing, clapping in a slow, sarcastic manner. His features were indistinct in the distance separating them. He leisurely jogged down the adjacent stone stairs past orange lantanas and mauve chaste trees toward her. *Shouldn't they be more concerned that I will escape and tell someone?*

Allowing the edge of her skirt to drop over her minuscule underwear, Emmi came to a stop. Her confusion grew when the guard approached, withdrawing a chilled bottle of water he had grabbed earlier for himself from one of the pockets on his cargo pants. Holding the drink out with one hand, his other clamped around a stubby security baton.

Finding his apprehension of her hysterical, Emilia managed a squeak of appreciation as she took the bottle. Her hand shaking as she held the icy beverage to her dry lips, windpipe burning she guzzled the drink inelegantly. She needed to believe this was all a foolish mistake.

"Miss Sondra, please. If you would accompany me," the guard implored, his expression tinged with judgment. "Your fiancé is expecting you."

Emilia bristled and took a step back. Increasing the distance between herself and the guard, she said, "Not Sondra. Most certainly not here presuming to meet a fiancé."

"How modern of you. A lover, then?" From behind her, the man from the concrete balcony spoke with a rich timbre as he neared them.

Emilia gaped. *Her? A lover? How presumptuous.* Turning around quickly to protest, she opened her mouth, but had no time to speak before seeing the look of confusion cross the man's face. His humor faded, eyes stiffened into a shocked stare, and his lips parted ever so slightly. For a brief moment, they simply held each other's gaze, both trying to figure out what happened and who the other was.

Regaining control of himself, the man spoke first, "Where are my manners? I'm Vincenzo." He leaned in to place a kiss on the throbbing vein in her wrist. Despite her reservations about the whole situation, the polished smoothness of the gesture sent goosebumps up her forearms.

"Have you gone mad?" Emilia ripped her hand from his loose grasp, unnerved by her reaction to his touch.

"You ask me if I've gone crazy?" Vincenzo deadpanned. "*Mia cara*, I wasn't the one doing the forty-yard dash on my lawn."

Vincenzo searched her face for any trace of deceit, from finely plucked brows to small upturned nose resting above parted wet lips. His brows furrowed slightly, eyes searching her face.

"Forgive me for staring, but you bear an uncanny resemblance to someone I know." He paused before straightening his countenance. "If you'll excuse me a minute?" At Emilia's nod, he snapped his fingers to catch the attention of the guard nearest him and instructed the man to call the chauffeur over.

The driver sauntered to Vincenzo's position, reluctantly joining him.

Vincenzo immediately set about scolding the man in Italian. "You imbecile!" His volume rose as he demanded to know how this mistake was made. "Who the hell is she?"

"She approached the shuttle like she knew it was for her. She looked like the woman whose picture you sent to me. I assumed she was Miss Perric," the driver replied with his shoulders shrugged, uneasy with the direction the conversation was taking. He was hesitant to tell Vincenzo about the angry woman who looked rather similar to Emilia who he'd left at the airport. Instead, he shifted gears. "Now that I get a good look at her, she looks like one of Strazzo's call girls," the driver said, scraping at a possible reason for his lack of due diligence.

Vincenzo stared at the man, torn between smacking him upside the head and agreeing with him. "Ridiculous. She nearly wet herself when I touched her wrist." He continued to appraise the brunette as her eyes warily met his.

Emilia listened as the men argued in Italian, searching for an explanation to all of this. Their conversation reached a fevered pitch before she interrupted them with the facts, shocking them with her knowledge of Italian. "Gentlemen. I understand this is quite the quandary. However, it's abundantly clear I'm not this Miss Perric person you've mistaken me for."

"You speak Italian?" the driver stuttered. His face flamed red. His countenance sheepish as he recollected referring to her as a prostitute moments before.

"Half-wit," Vincenzo muttered. "Go find out what's happened to Sondra. At once."

"Yes, sir." The driver scurried off, relieved to leave the scene.

Turning to Emmi, Vincenzo tried to patch up the chauffer's giant mistake. "My apologies, I shouldn't have presumed and excluded you from the conversation. You said your name was? Would you care to sit a moment? I appreciate the sun, but not its full zenith." His gaze pointed to a pavilion overgrown with foliage in the middle of the yard not far from where they stood.

"It's Mrs. Patric, and certainly, please lead the way." Matching his pace, she crossed the soft grass, taking the seat he offered. *His eyes remind me of a warm, finely flavored cognac.*

Virile, whispered her biological clock.

Oh, shut it Canadian bacon. Next thing you know, you'll be talking about flowing hair and Fabio.

"If you'll allow me to explain, I—" Emilia stopped mid-sentence as a stately brunette stepped through the gate meters from where she and Vincenzo sat. The woman had clearly aged gracefully, her slightly graying hair only adding to her aura of confidence. Emmi watched as she crossed the distance, blinking as the woman thrust a jeweled hand laden with a three-carat diamond ring into her purview.

"Please allow me to introduce myself. I'm Vitoria." Emmi took her hand in a warm shake. "The guards alerted me to your arrival. I thought you might be more comfortable with a woman present. It seems you were mistaken for our Sondra?" The woman peered closer at Emmi. "You do look very similar to her, except for the eyes." Vitoria straightened and patted Emmi's hand before letting it go.

These people are nuttier than Grandma's Christmas pound cake. Still, there's something about this woman I like. "My name is Emilia Patric."

At the exchange of names, a warm smile crept over Vitoria's face. Initially, she thought the coltishly slender woman had slipped by her staff and son with her feminine wiles, but this one didn't have the same stench of desperation the other women had.

Emilia continued, "I was about to expound on what I think happened. I called for the hotel shuttle while at the airport. I went to collect it in the spot assigned by the hotel administrator, which is where I found your driver sitting. Nothing untoward, a mistake which is easily rectified. I'll call a cab and be on my way," she said while pulling her cell phone out of her purse. "Sorry to have troubled you."

Vitoria paused, watching as Emilia and Vincenzo regarded one another. Every inch his father's son, Vitoria loved every crease of his face. Her son had grown into a fine man, deserving of every happiness.

"You'll have to forgive us. We were expecting Sondra, Vincenzo's fiancée." Vitoria looked to Vincenzo, as she spoke the untruth they used to deter unsuitable women who'd set their sights on Strazzo. "Besides the resemblance, you bear a similar last name."

Emilia returned Vitoria's smile politely. "Nothing to forgive. This was my fault, and sadly it's not the first time I've been mistaken for someone else. I really should be going." Emilia looked across the grounds, her eyes settling with trepidation on the dogs that munched casually on her favorite pair of shoes.

"What a lovely scarf," Vitoria stated, delicately reaching out to touch the soft silk.

Emilia's attention returned to the conversation at hand. "Oh, thank you." She looked down at the scarf around her neck and touched her fingers to it. "My husband gave it to me as an anniversary gift."

Vitoria's eyebrows raised slightly at this bit of information. *Emilia Patric is already spoken for.* Slyly glancing in Vincenzo's direction, she noticed her son hiding a look of disappointment. "Are you certain you wouldn't like to join us for supper, Emilia?" Vitoria asked. Her curiosity outdone by her hospitality.

"I couldn't impose," Emilia stated. After spending so much time alone during the last few years, she was becoming aware of her discomfort at currently being in the company of many people.

"Nonsense," Vitoria waved her arms dismissively. "I offered. Therefore, the imposition, mine. How can I impose upon myself? This is not logical." Vitoria, unwilling to take no for an answer, pasted a slight pout upon her otherwise flawless face.

Emilia didn't want to offend, but the idea of spending the start of her vacation in the company of strangers—especially this despicably magnetic Vincenzo character—wasn't one she relished in any sense. She glared at Vincenzo, her eyes resting on his countenance.

Vitoria assessed Emilia, noting the tension across the woman's shoulders, before looking to her son. His immovable gaze regarded Emilia so long it was positively improper. *Interesting.*

"Emilia, you simply must stay." Glancing toward the family dogs still happily destroying Emmi's shoes, Vitoria added, "Think of it as an apology for any inconvenience this mistake has caused." Then looking briefly at her son, "And, perhaps, an unexpected chance to make new friends."

Vincenzo's gaze finally broke away from Emmi to meet with his mother's. A common thought with the woman who had known him his entire life. It had been a good, long time since he regarded any woman in the way he had Emilia.

Emilia mulled over Vitoria's words, reflecting how her life was often derailed by unplanned events, and how her success rate for surviving them thus far was one hundred percent. "I'll need to make a call first. My schedule is somewhat inflexible."

Vitoria gestured toward the back door of their home. "Wonderful! We have a landline indoors if you'd prefer to use it?"

Glancing at her cell phone, Emmi realized her service was not the greatest at this expansive estate. "If it's not too much trouble. I'll need to collect my shoes first." Emilia looked downward at the high arch of her foot.

At the mention of her shoes, Vincenzo's gaze resumed its previously traveled path, and traversed her golden limbs to the tip of her nude-polished toes, realizing belatedly he'd ogled her legs. "Go ahead and use the phone. I'll get your shoes."

Emilia crossed the paving stones and entered the foyer of the home. Classic architectural lines paired with warm, tasteful décor graced the entrance. It was accentuated by graceful pillars of wintry stone. Unable to resist, she circled the pillar and passed a hand over the marble's cool surface with interest and admiration. She hadn't seen marble such as this since she toured the quarries in the Apuan Alps of Italy.

Emmi reluctantly tore her gaze away from the support columns to search for the phone. Spotting the ornate oak desk, she padded barefoot across the cool tiles to place her call. She removed the ivory-carved handpiece from its cradle and dialed, waiting for the grainy, low-key tone to connect her with her intended receiver.

"Hello, it's Emilia… Yes, I'm fine… No, not yet. There was a bit of confusion with the hotel shuttle. Shall we go over the meeting details tonight?" Emmi let out a sigh at what the other person said. "Yes, I am supposed to be on vacation, aren't I? Fine… Okay… I said fine! I've been invited to supper, anyhow… Good lord, I am most certainly not getting an itch scratched. Honestly, Danny, you're perfectly perverted. I'll fill you in tomorrow."

Emilia turned as the call ended, startled to see Vincenzo with her shoes in hand. *How much of the conversation had he overheard?* She studied his fastidious appearance—his leonine bearing, the cut of his jaw, the arrogance in his expression conveyed a man used to getting his way. They stood staring at one another, an electric silence between them as they sized one another up.

"I trust you found what you needed." His manner shifted as he handed off her half-chewed, barely wearable shoes.

"Yes, thank you." Her heart slammed against her ribs as his fingers grazed hers unintentionally. She dipped downward to cover the rise of color in her face, hiding the wince as she attempted to force the moist shoe on her foot.

Seeing her wobble, Vincenzo closed the distance and offered his arm to allow her to steady herself. Taking the other shoe, he knelt and pushed the soggy mule onto her foot with an unsteady hand. *Married woman. Off-limits,* blared a warning somewhere in the back of his mind.

Emilia stood stock still as Vincenzo's warm hands gently encircled her ankle and guided her foot into the shoe. She became suddenly aware that his touch was the first caress she had felt since the death of her husband. His head was so close to her legs that his dark hair whispered against her thighs, sending a shiver up her spine. *Don't look up. Don't look up,* she silently pleaded with him. Closing her eyes, the flames of an indecent thought created the first lick of an unquenchable fire.

He looked up. His line of sight was directly in line with her sex. *Dear god.* Vincenzo stood hastily, eyes flitting like a captured bird as he tried to unsee the seen. With aplomb worthy of royalty itself, he changed the subject to a much safer topic. "You seemed interested in the marble earlier. Would you like to know more about its origin?"

Emilia blushed, thinking he must have seen her caress the cool, smooth stone and realizing at the same time that meant he'd heard her entire conversation, including the part about a supposed itch that needed scratching. "I hope I haven't offended you. The columns reminded me of the stonework from a quarry I toured in Italy."

"Not at all. You have keen eyes. My father brought the marble in after he made his first million. This was taken from the quarry where he worked as a youth. He would have appreciated your admiration of his painstaking project."

Emilia reached out to touch Vincenzo's forearm, a silly whim overtaking her as she gently tapped one toe on the base of the pillar. "I hope you're not one of those people who take this stuff for granite." She looked up at him through her lashes to see if he'd caught her pun, a sly half-smile playing on her lips.

Vincenzo looked down into her gold-flecked eyes with all seriousness. "Emilia Patric, I do believe you are flirting with me. With puns, no less."

Seized by the urge to trace the outline of her lips, forgetting momentarily the Mrs. portion of her name, he pulled her close. His hands at her back, he kissed her like the ocean overtakes a small stone. Wet, rough, tumultuous, and thoroughly glorious.

She returned his kiss, her hands creeping upward around his neck. Yielding to him, her lips parted as her tongue darted out to explore his mouth.

"*Mio dio*," he whispered as he unsteadily broke off their kiss, not trusting himself to be able to resist pressing her against the phone stand and follow wherever the current of passion led them.

Emmi disentangled herself from his embrace, shaking slightly. Her knees felt as though they might give out at any moment. More flustered than aroused at the memory of his supposed fiancée, she blurted, "I'm sorry. I didn't mean for that to happen."

Before Vincenzo could respond, he noticed a slight movement in the doorway. Vitoria stood with a hand over her mouth. Her eyes accusing, he was thankful that Emilia's back was toward her. Vincenzo cleared his throat. "Is there something I could help you with, Mama?"

Ignoring the palpable tension in the room, Vitoria came forward. "I came to ask if both of you would like to walk before the evening meal?" Switching her gaze from her son to Emmi, she continued, "There's a nearby nature preserve I like to visit in the early evenings."

"Yes," Emilia agreed breathlessly, blushing from neck to crown. She needed to escape Vincenzo's penetrating stare, to pretend the soul-searing kiss she shared with the man never happened. She couldn't even begin to imagine what Vitoria must think of her.

Breaking eye contact with his mother, Vincenzo glanced at the large clock on the foyer wall. "My apologies, Mama. I need to make a few phone calls."

Emilia watched as he retreated up the curved stairway, feeling a mix of relief and disappointment. She lost sight of him behind the gradual arc of the stair wall and let out a breath she didn't know she'd been holding. *What was she thinking? He's engaged!*

Ten minutes later, Vincenzo watched Emilia from the balcony of the second floor. Runners replaced her expensive heels. Her silken curtain of dark hair was under a ball cap bearing a hockey team logo. An eager grin was on her face as she and his mother drove off.

He thought of his soon-to-be ex-wife, Isabella. She would never have enjoyed such a bucolic pastime. Nor would she have told silly jokes. She'd always been so serious, so reserved.

Thoughts returning to the woman who'd suddenly walked into his life, Vincenzo dwelled on their kiss. Little shocked him, but Mrs. Emilia Patric floored him when she French kissed him with a wild, all-consuming passion in his mother's foyer. He felt a smirk cross his face as he touched his lips.

"It's as if we're not in the city anymore." Emilia looked around with wide-eyed appreciation. She was genuinely pleased to find an expanse of forest within Houston proper, not expecting the gritty city to have a hidden copse of lush trees with glossy green leaves and shaded wooden walkways that led to still ponds. "Goodness, there's even a few turtles here." She pointed to one, as it soaked up the generous sunrays of the day. Squirrels skittered across the ground, chittering a familiar refrain as a bird swooped from one treetop to the next.

"It's a gem for certain," Vitoria responded with a smile as they approached the trailhead. "There are roughly eighteen acres of land with several walking paths and bridges that branch out to the most delicious views… if you know where to look." Vitoria walked toward an interpretive sign that gave an overview of the layout of the sanctuary.

As the women walked the planks enjoying the reprieve from the heat, Vitoria searched for a way to broach the subject that burned in her mind. *How did Emilia Patric—billionaire and CEO of one of the largest research firms topside of the US border—end up taking a shuttle to our house?*

A voracious reader of Business Fortune magazine, Vitoria would have glossed over the piece if it weren't for the powerful picture the woman presented. As she read on, she felt pride in her fellow womankind. The article had discussed how Emilia outstripped her male counterparts and carved a niche for herself in a male-dominated arena. Not an easy feat, as Vitoria was all too well aware of. It was as though having breasts and indoor plumbing somehow made one incapable of such accomplishments.

Rather than spill all she knew, Vitoria tried to open up the topic casually. "Your face is familiar. Did you grow up in the Houston area? Where might I have seen you prior? I'm certain I have."

Emmi blanched, wondering if Vitoria knew who she was. She didn't like discussing herself with strangers, never knowing if they had some sort of angle. But she relaxed when she considered the improbability of Vitoria actually having heard of her or her company. "Doubtful. I was born in Canada. Lived abroad for a few years, then settled on the coast after I met my husband."

Searching Emilia's hand, Vitoria wondered about the lack of a ring on her finger despite the fact she had mentioned her husband twice now. Instead, she kept her thoughts to herself, trying to recall the article. *It mentioned the woman's husband, but what had it said?* She did remember reading that it wasn't Emilia's husband's money that made her a billionaire. Emilia was a unicorn—she was one of a handful of self-made female billionaires.

"How exciting. Any children? You've met one of my three sons—the eldest—who recently received the reins of our family business. My middle son is on tour at the moment, while the youngest of my sons is a hapless boy with a heart of gold."

Ignoring the question about whether she had any children, Emilia's ears perked at the talk of business, always keeping her ear to the ground for opportunities to mentor new business owners. "I may know a few people who could help."

"With what? The hapless boy, or the others?" Vitoria laughed. "What is it you do for work?" She waited to see if the woman at her side would boast or take the road of humility.

"I work for a privately funded corporation," Emilia answered elusively before changing the subject. "Vincenzo doesn't strike me as someone who will struggle in the business realm. I shouldn't think you'll need to worry too much once he gets his feet under him."

"No, but he's relatively new to being CEO. His father and I ran the company together up until his death, and I'm getting on in years." Vitoria looked away, wringing her hands together. "I fear business is changing. Technology was the death of many of our business counterparts. So, I know a change is required. He doesn't see it yet, I don't think."

Emilia smiled, thinking of Buridan's principle she used to help merger clients decide to take a risk. "Perhaps you could help him to see the need by using an analogy. A donkey, equally hungry and thirsty, stands an equal distance between hay and water. Unable to decide which to go to first, it waits so long it dies. If it had forethought, it would drink the water then eat the hay. Similarly, businesses must act to stay relevant."

"Yes, very true. One must constantly shift their paradigm."

"Agreed. If it's not too personal of a question, how did Vincenzo react when you asked to retire?" Emilia wondered if he felt tied to a life he hadn't chosen for himself.

"He knew it would come to this. However, the timing is poor," Vitoria confided.

Emilia considered what little she knew of the man who had stood beside her examining the marble, to what she knew of his character thus far. "Sounds like there's a backstory. I understand if you don't wish to share." Emmi backpedaled her way out of the personal territory she found herself ensnared in.

"Yes, there is more to tell, but it's not my story to share. Perhaps he will tell you himself," Vitoria said, thinking how her son's gaze had hungrily followed the woman at her side, and how shocked she was to find him kissing her. She eyed her companion and decided she liked Mrs. Emilia Patric very much. It was easy to see why the magazine touted her as one of the top twenty women in business to watch over the next five years.

The casual walk among the beautiful greenery helped Emilia feel more at ease in

Vitoria's presence. Emilia wondered about Vitoria's husband and what had happened to him. Vitoria didn't look old enough to be a widow. Then again, neither did Emilia, and yet here she was.

***

At the dinner table, the three of them chatted easily about superficial topics such as a movie they'd all recently watched and the typical hot September they were having in Houston. Emilia was surprised to discover herself feeling so comfortable amongst strangers. She enjoyed the loving and familiar looks that she witnessed between Vincenzo and his mother. Emmi was used to eating her meals on the run, often alone and rushed. This was much more gratifying. The food hadn't even been served and here she was, truly relishing the moment.

"You *must* visit Galveston beach while you're in Texas," Vitoria said.

"I have to admit, it's been a while since I allowed myself to relax by the waves." Emmi thought back to her honeymoon with her husband on the beach of Jamaica, but was quickly brought back to the conversation with Vitoria's next question.

"I don't believe you ever said why you chose to come to Texas?"

Hearing a timer drift out the open window, Emilia was relieved to avoid the topic of work.

Vitoria raised a finger as she spoke. "Oh, that'll be our supper." She rushed off into the house and returned a short time later carrying a pan roasted Napoletana pizza topped with brightly colored roasted vegetables. She placed it on the table before them, the aroma instantly causing Emilia's mouth to water.

As she took her first bite of the homemade delicacy, Emmi took note of its richly flavored sauce of fresh-pureed tomatoes, garlic, and oregano. She had to refrain herself from scarfing the food hastily and ungraciously. Besides it being delicious, she had missed lunch during her flight. For once, she was not thinking about her work or eating merely to meet a need.

Slowing herself down with a sip of her beverage, Emilia enjoyed the lightly oaked white wine. Her well-vetted palate homed in on the notes of stone fruit and honey, and she found herself smiling more than she had in the last five years.

The trio continued to talk between bites as the topic casually shifted to Vincenzo's father. Hearing how Vincenzo spoke of his father and their early morning fishing trips left Emmi relaxed, but melancholic.

"What about your family, Emilia?" Vitoria asked inevitably.

"Mother passed relatively young. Though, I recall her kindness in particular. Always a kind word on her lips. A hand out to share her food. She had a gift for making anyone feel welcome. In what little I've seen this evening, you remind me of her a great deal, Vitoria."

Vitoria blushed. "Oh, shush now. You're just buttering me up."

"Life is fleeting—one must say the nice things they feel to the persons we admire. Praising them to others doesn't benefit the deserving party," Emilia said, a twinge of regret in her voice as she wished she could have told her mother how much she admired her spirit of self-sacrifice.

"I think you are wise beyond your years, dear girl," Vitoria remarked. Lifting her glass with appreciation, she took a drink.

"It's clear you don't know Mama very well." Vincenzo smirked. "She never stood at the top of your stairs yelling at the top of her lungs to get your dirty underwear into the laundry bin."

Emilia laughed as Vitoria reached over to smack Vincenzo. Their easy way with one another was infectious in its simplicity. "Maybe you shouldn't have left your little superhero underwear lying so carelessly in the middle of the floor for the dog to eat."

"Perhaps I put them in the bin, and the dog took them out," Vincenzo quipped with humor. "In retrospect, I wish I thought to blame the dog sooner."

Their continued camaraderie, accompanied by the touch of light fragrance from the violet-blue wisteria clinging to the pergola, made the evening all the more enjoyable.

As Vitoria excused herself to clear some of the dishes, Vincenzo withdrew the chair next to Emmi and slipped in. "You surprise me, Emilia."

"Why is that?" She repositioned her chair to face him. Legs crossed at the ankles in a relaxed position. For once, she hadn't felt like a stranger. It was an odd thing to be a billionaire—to be a part of something larger than one could imagine. Having the freedom to do anything and everything while also feeling truly free just did not seem to go together. Instead, the reality was having to guard yourself neurotically. No one was as they appeared. There was always an angle or scheme to part you from your hard-earned coin.

"You seem to fit well here with us." He leaned back, crossing his arms over his chest. "Tell me, who sent you?"

"Pardon me?" Emilia looked to the chirping chickadees, ruffling and fluffing themselves in a fountain, their birdsong echoing through the area. She was not paying much attention, assuming Vincenzo teased as he had before.

He topped off Emmi's wine as his voice became more insistent. "I'm certain you do. You're too sophisticated to come from this picturesque village you describe as home. Less affluent people don't fit in with millionaires. So, I ask again, who sent you?"

Pulling her hand away from his firm grasp, Emilia's eyes narrowed. "This line of questioning is distasteful, Vincenzo. If I discover your work is involved with mine, I'll let you know. The rest is none of your business."

Emmi took a plate in hand and stood before she gave him a lip-whipping he'd never forget. She couldn't decide which irritated her more—his inappropriate line of questioning, or the assumption she was after his billfold. As if she were somehow incapable of earning her own money. *The absolute nerve.* She toyed with the idea of having a couple of Chinook helicopters dump a superyacht worth more than his net income on his front lawn.

"Please, it's not our custom for guests to clear the table," Vincenzo instructed with another show of toxic masculinity, lifting his wrist to draw attention to his diamond-encrusted watch.

Too bad it's not customary for you to act like a gentleman, Emilia thought, staring back at him as though he were an ant who'd soon meet his fate under her heel.

Vitoria watched from a discreet distance as her son rudely interrogated their guest. *What on earth has brought on my son's boorish behavior?* This was not like her Vincenzo. Seeing irritation on Emilia's face, Vitoria chose to make her presence known before the pair came to blows.

Clearing her throat, she stepped forward. "I'm so glad you decided to stay. We never have time for family meals." Vitoria steered the conversation in a lighter direction while she gathered more plates from the table.

"Us neither, it seems," Emilia said, eyes cast downward. Lifting her chin again, she added, "Though, Thanksgiving is popular at my house—I make a mean pumpkin pie."

"You cook?" Vitoria exclaimed, delighted at the possibility of finding a fellow food-experience hunter, hoping to learn more about her guest.

"Candidly speaking, there was a time I didn't realize I needed to bake the filling in a lemon pie," Emmi remarked with a smirk, continuing to help her host to clear plates.

"If you'd like to share, I'm listening. You're a compelling orator."

"And, I think you're being too polite. Though, it is funny, so I'll indulge myself. I promised to bring a pie for our graduation ceremony. Made the graham cracker crust, poured the filling in. Whipped up the meringue for the topping. Feeling quite pleased with myself, I popped that sucker into the fridge, imagining the filling solidified like gelatin, and took it to the gathering the next day."

"Oh, *no*," Vitoria gasped, covering her mouth to stifle a giggle.

"Oh, *yes*." Emilia giggled at herself. "I didn't realize my error until I heard someone shout, 'What the hell? Who made this? It's not even cooked!'" Emmi slapped her hand on her own forehead. "I watched in horror as the meringue slid off the entire pie. I was so embarrassed."

"And did you own up to being the one who 'baked' it?" Vitoria used her fingers to make air quotes.

"I didn't even collect the dish I'd brought it in afterward."

Vitoria erupted into laughter as she turned for the house, Emilia following behind. Their laughter continued until they stepped into the kitchen.

"This space is amazing." Emilia rushed forward, twirling to take in the entire room. Her gaze darted from the antique-style industrial hood overtop a dual gas range to the multi-colored stonework opposite the fireplace. An eight-seat, hand-hewn solid wood table similar in color to the hazelnut support beams tied the aesthetic lines together against the pale, cream color of the walls. Parsley, basil, and rosemary hung cheerily in bundles by the wide bank of windows. Their frames were outlined in ivy, giving the space a hearth-like smell that reminded her of a natural foods supermarket.

"It's among the features I'm most proud of in this house." Vitoria beamed. "My late husband and I shared in the preparation of many meals here." Her face took on a wistful cast, the shine of her eyes brighter for the tears that clung there.

"You must miss him," Emilia said with a gentleness born of experience. How often had she seen Mason in her mind's eye, hunched over their countertop as he'd worked on their kitchen? How many times had she collapsed on the floor crying, realizing he wasn't really there?

"Yes. Though, I don't miss his vigorous overuse of garlic. I am safe from vampires for many years," Vitoria added with a wry laugh.

"Husbands are funny, aren't they? With their little quirks. Mason eats everything with hot sauce and jalapenos. Won't touch a vegetable." Emilia grinned. Even five years later, she struggled to speak of him in the past tense. Mason would always be with her, even if just in memory.

"Ah, yes. This elusive husband you speak of, is he here in Texas?" Vitoria asked.

Emilia thought of Mason's ashes above her mantle. "No. He's in Canada."

"He must be heading up the company in your absence. What was it you do again? You said you were in private industry but didn't expound," Vitoria continued, wanting to pry further, but restraining herself.

"I didn't, did I?" Aware she'd done it again. Emilia moved a few dishes around on the counter, carefully forming a response in her mind *Do I want to go there? Once spoken, the words don't go back in again.* Sort of like meeting long-lost relatives, once you meet them, you can't unmeet them.

"Vitoria, I—" Emilia started. The words stuck in her throat as she faced her host.

"If it helps—" Vitoria said at the same time. They both laughed nervously before Vitoria continued. "I recognized you from Business Fortune magazine. I suspected when you said your name, but wanted to confirm before I said anything."

Emilia chewed her lower lip, giving the woman a small smile. "Thank you for your discretion, then. I'm certain Vincenzo thinks I'm a money honey out to fleece him of his meager millions, while your driver made no bones about labeling me as a high-class call girl."

"What?" Vitoria squawked, mortified that her guest had been ill-treated two different times. Her attention became divided as one of the topics of their conversation entered the hallway and headed their way.

"These days, I prefer the term harridan over honey or harlot. I spend a lot less time on my backside that way," Emilia snarked, then gave Vitoria an it's-all-good smile.

Vitoria laughed brightly, happy that Emilia seemed to be joking about it rather than taking any serious offense.

"It seems I've missed something," Vincenzo said.

"Nothing but a little girl talk. That said, I think it's time I turn in for the evening." Victoria covered her smile with a hand as her mouth was overtaken by a yawn.

Emilia folded the tea towel she used and placed it on the counter. "And, I think it's high time I made arrangements to get a cab. Thank you ever so much for the warmth and generosity of your hospitality. Not to mention, making this trip to Houston uniquely memorable, Vitoria."

"Nonsense. Vincenzo can take you back to your hotel," Vitoria remarked, not waiting to hear his reply. She hoped her son might use the time to explore the undercurrents that surged between himself and Emilia.

Emilia cringed inwardly, but maintained a neutral face. *Ugh. He and I could barely speak civilly to one another at supper, even after sharing an unbelievable kiss. I'd rather have a root canal. Or a pap smear.*

"Of course, Mama. I wouldn't dream of sending our wayward guest home alone," he teased. "She's liable to land up in Tulsa."

Emilia was confused by his sudden warmth again. *This guy flip flops more than a beach bum's favorite shoes.*

As Vitoria hugged her guest goodbye, she whispered, "*In bocca al lupo*, my dear."

Into the wolf's mouth I go, indeed. Recognizing the phrasing as a wish for good luck, Emilia responded under her breath, "*Crepi il lupo.*" *I crack the wolf. May it die.*

"Should I meet you in the driveway, Vincenzo?" Emilia shared one last look with Vitoria, who bid them good night once more.

"We'll take my car. I'll have our man bring the car around." Vincenzo withdrew a small device from his pocket and sent off the request.

With them both waiting for the car and no excuse to separate, Vincenzo and Emilia stood uncomfortably in silence where Vitoria had left them in the kitchen.

"Why don't we move to the living room while we wait?" Vincenzo attempted to break the awkwardness. Leading the way, he added, "You'll have to give me your address. Perhaps we'll meet again under different circumstances." *At the very least, I'll know where to address the restraining order*, he thought.

"Doubtful. I have an aversion to handsome, arrogant men. Your case seems especially terminal," Emilia shot off without restraint, shocked to hear her thoughts spoken aloud.

"You found me charmingly arrogant. Yet, you liked me," a familiar voice intoned.

Emilia's gaze looked over Vincenzo's shoulder toward the voice, landing first on the gorgeous woman bearing a striking resemblance to herself who stood at the man's side. *The fiancée*, Emilia thought. *Was she the woman from the shuttle mishap?* It was all coming together now.

Vincenzo turned toward the new arrivals. "Aren't you supposed to be in France, Strazzo?" His brother should be halfway across the Atlantic Ocean by now, or at least pants deep in some flight attendant. Acknowledging Emilia's doppelganger, he said, "Nice to see you, Sondra."

What an odd way to greet one's fiancée, Emilia thought. And yet, at the mention of Sondra's name, she felt a tug in her gut. *Is that…jealousy?*

"Emilia, my youngest brother, Strazzo, and Miss Sondra Perric. Strazzo, Sondra, may I introduce Mrs. Emilia Patric."

Emilia managed to peel her eyes off Sondra and address the man. Eyes widening in recognition, she spat out, "You!" *Not-Dante, here, in the flesh.* "Should've known you two were related," she said, motioning between the brothers. *Could this night get any worse? I can't decide which of them I hate more.*

"Nice to see you again, Miss Patric." Strazzo leered at Emmi in an obvious way, wondering how she knew his brother.

"I see you two already know one another." Vincenzo's brow lifted slightly, catching Emilia's scathing gaze at his youngest brother, one he wasn't entirely unfamiliar with.

"I would've made my flight if it weren't for Ms. Klutz, here," Strazzo scoffed. "And Sondra was left at the airport by that hack you call a chauffeur thanks to her as well. She seems to enjoy stirring up trouble." Strazzo sniffed haughtily, reaching out to clasp Sondra's hand possessively.

In the heat of her defense rising, Emmi missed the odd action between two people who would soon be in-laws. "Oh, please. You were already late when you manhandled me into an upright position after tearing the front half of my dress down. Then you had the gall to lie to me about your name!"

"You all but invited me back to your hotel room." Strazzo watched his brother's face for some reaction, as Sondra looked on with a shock of her own.

Glaring at Not-Dante, Emilia snorted. "You're a despicable liar, Dante. Or should I say *Strazzo*? I offered a drink as a gesture of gratitude, nothing further. I should've slapped you harder. Maybe it would've jarred your skull meat into action."

Circling the room with a strut, Strazzo stopped midstride. "How could you not know who I am?"

"Oh, I know who you are without a fraction of a doubt. You're a spoiled child with an enormous ego; a veritable Peter Pan," Emilia blurted out, thinking of a psychological syndrome by the name.

"Are you seriously going to stand there and insult me in my own house?" Strazzo stepped forward.

"Your house? My left foot in your arse, you pompous ass. You're, what, twenty-five? And still sponging off your mother? Grow a pair, see the world, contribute."

Vincenzo stared at Emilia and Strazzo, as they stood nose to nose. He coughed to cover the boisterous laugh that had sprung from his mouth, thinking of Emilia as a small rabbit baring her teeth, though her assessment of Strazzo was one hundred percent spot-on.

"It appears you two have some unfinished business you need to talk through. As fun as this is to watch, I think I'll go check on the car," Vincenzo said.

Sondra side eyed Strazzo, watching as the latter postured ridiculously. "I think I'll head upstairs. It's been a long day. Though, for the record, my cash is on her." She high-fived the air toward Emilia on her way upstairs—an action that Emilia returned.

Maybe I do like this woman, Emilia thought as a smirk tugged at the left corner of her mouth.

Strazzo paused in front of the fireplace to move a photo of his father atop the mantle, his eyes on the door as he waited for Vincenzo and Sondra to leave before he closed the gap between himself and Emilia.

"Such passion, Emilia." Strazzo suddenly pressed himself against her, changing his tactic to one that usually worked.

Emilia stiffened. Her nose permeated with the smell of an overpowering cologne. His chiseled features inches from hers, as his hands traveled dangerously close to the curve of her bottom.

"Are you sure you don't want *me* to take you back to the hotel?"

"Quite sure." She sidestepped his groping hand nimbly, circling behind an armchair as he chased her around the room.

Strazzo pulled himself straight as he puffed out his chest. "I'm Strazzo, baby. Everyone wants a piece of this action. Or don't you read the news?"

Such hubris. Emilia wondered if she should tell him precisely who she was. By news metrics alone, he was chump change in her ashtray.

Finding herself cornered, Strazzo trapped her in his arms. Emilia's eyes locked with the shocked countenance of Vincenzo who had returned to let her know the car was ready, just as Strazzo's lips crushed down on hers forcefully.

Vincenzo stared at Emilia encircled in the arms of his brother. He'd been so stunned he'd simply backed out of the room. What else could he have done? *Had she kissed Strazzo at the airport the way she kissed me in the office? Does she make a habit of kissing random men?* Vincenzo's heart plunged involuntarily.

He returned to the car and angrily shuffled the baggage to make room in the back seat in case Strazzo insisted on joining them.

A fraction of a second later, Emilia burst from the house, her garments looking disheveled. She thought about mentioning how Strazzo had cornered her, but decided against it. It just felt too awkward and presumptuous to bring up. *Thirty more minutes of my time, and I'll never need to see either of them again, so it really doesn't matter, does it?*

Taking a steadying breath, she rounded the car and took her position in the passenger seat. With a look in Vincenzo's direction, she found his profile illuminated by the soft glow of the driver console. Her line of sight traced the small scar on the bridge of his nose, thinking how it added to the ruggedness of his features.

Interrupting her stare, he asked, "What hotel are you staying at?"

Emmi told him and he deftly typed it into his navigation system. His left hand gripped the wheel casually. A lean index finger guided the wheel, his thumb at its base as his hand rested atop his leg while he exited their grounds and put the car through its paces.

Emmi shifted to better observe the night sky, reviewing the events of the day. Dining with Vincenzo's family left her feeling raw. Their ease with one another reminded her of what she'd lost. She avoided relationships. *I even reneged on pet ownership*, she thought as a small wirehaired Jack Russell mix bounded down the street. She'd practically become a shut-in. Work was all she did. No wonder Danny hounded her so fiercely to get out of the office on time in the evenings. She made a mental note to adopt a dog once her foundation was up and running.

"I would like to apologize for how I behaved at supper." Vincenzo's voice broke their shared silence. "It was a day among hectic days. I shouldn't have presumed you were anything other than a traveler who'd made an error."

Contemplating Vitoria's brief mention of his undisclosed stress, Emmi said, "I'm sorry as well. You must think me dense for disrupting your day with what could have easily been avoided had I checked with your driver. I'm beginning to wonder if I'm cursed though, meeting both you and your brother on the same day." She tried salting the strain between them with humor.

Instead, Vincenzo bristled. He felt testy as he thought about her likely reaction to his brother's lips on hers, thinking she would reciprocate as every other woman had in the years he and Strazzo had competed for women.

"Strazzo picks up a stray every other week. All that's left is your seduction, then the inevitable discard," he said harshly, presuming she was attracted to his younger brother.

Emilia folded her arms across her body and seethed at his thinly veiled insinuation she would willingly be another of Strazzo's discarded sluts. She flicked an expletive off her tongue and stopped herself from cursing him out with every colorful adjective she knew. "If you think every woman responds to Strazzo's tactics, you're wrong. I am not every woman, and—"

Vincenzo interrupted her mid-sentence. "You're a poor liar, Emilia Patric. I saw you. You looked quite cozy. It's fine," he said, throwing his hands up briefly before returning them to the wheel. "You don't need to explain anything. As you so clearly pointed out earlier, your business is none of mine."

Emilia glared at him as he twisted her words from earlier, her eyes pricking with tears as her voice shook. "I don't care what it looked like, Vincenzo. I am still very much in love with my dead husband."

"Pardon me?" Vincenzo grunted in disbelief. "You don't look old enough to be widowed."

"How does one *look* like a widow, Vincenzo? Should I have a thin frame with all my bones showing? Should I walk around like the living dead? Because trust me, that's how it feels!" Not one to cry easily, the buildup of the day's events prodded her, creating a rare trail of tears down her face.

"You never mentioned you were a widow," he replied quietly, her vulnerability taking the wind out of his argument. Her perceivable anguish snuffed his anger out completely.

"When would I have found the time? I was invited to dinner, not to sit on the couch with the therapist. It's not like it's something I go around advertising. It's painful, Vincenzo. Mentioning that my husband died in Afghanistan was not on the menu."

"Forgive me. I misspoke." He pulled out of traffic, stopping the car alongside the sidewalk to give her his full attention. Looking directly at her, he said, "I didn't know."

"Whatever you think of me, know you have it wrong, Vincenzo," she said softly. Her resolve cracking under the weight of her emotions.

Vincenzo sighed. "It seems we were both burdened by our assumption of one another." He reached into his chest pocket and grabbed a tissue to hand to her, his hand brushing hers in the process.

"I don't need this," she said, taking the small white square anyway. She dabbed it at the corner of her eyes with a forced laugh. She wanted nothing more than to be done with today and be back home where the days slid by predictably.

"Your mascara says otherwise," he chided gently, and reached to wipe away a stubborn dark smudge with his thumb. His gaze lingered on her lips, evoking the memory of how she'd kissed him earlier. *Like a drowning woman.*

"Better?" She turned her glossy, red-rimmed eyes toward him. She wondered at her mental state having confessed her love for a dead man to a stranger.

Her face holds a wounded look, he thought. She may have concealed the trail of tears with a dusting of powder, but it didn't erase the shattered look nor the sorrow that remained in her eyes.

"You're beautiful, but even more so when you cry." Overcome by an urge to kiss her again, but sensing her vulnerability, he kissed her forehead instead. His touch was gentle along the curve of her cheek. He reached out in the darkness. His hand dwarfed hers as he awkwardly squeezed it, refusing to let go. "Without sounding insensitive, could we start over?"

She held his hand, grateful to him for not needing to discuss her husband's death in minute detail. "I'd like that."

Pulling away from the curb, he rejoined the flow of traffic, sneaking an occasional look at his passenger.

She spoke first, squashing her instinct to mentally plan her upcoming week of work. It remained her only reprieve whenever grief reared its ugly head. "I meant to ask, what made you go electric?"

"It made sense. We're sitting on an oil crisis within fifty years. That, and the legroom."

"Here I believed you'd regale me with fables of how fast it went from zero to sixty and how maneuverable the car was," she taunted.

"This is last year's model. It reaches sixty between three and four seconds," he responded with a cheeky grin on his face.

"Slower than mine," she confessed, reeling herself in before she talked about her penchant for fast cars—classic and otherwise. "Sure, it's fast, but it's automatic. I like to drive stick," Emmi confessed. "Traveling through some of the mountainous regions on the island, I prefer more control."

"Are we still comparing cars?" he drawled.

Emilia smiled into the darkened interior of the car as their conversation flowed from one topic to the next, the mood shifting until a comfortable silence fell once more. Her thoughts scattered as she considered her widowed state, and the newfound attraction she felt to the man beside her—despite his upcoming nuptials.

"Penny for your thoughts, Emilia."

"I was thinking of the ocean. Your mother said I should see Galveston while I'm here. How far away is it?"

"Maybe an hour or so. Would you like to go?"

"If I'm not keeping you from anything. I'd love to wake up to the sound of the waves hitting the shore." Less than twenty-four hours away from her home, and she already yearned for the calm sound of the ocean lapping against the driftwood-strewn shorefront, while chocolate-colored mink scampered through jagged rock outcroppings.

Drat. I didn't fill the feeders, she thought, her mind on the bronze-plumed hummingbirds, which flitted and darted through the sky before they dove to sample suet and syrup from the troughs she'd put out for them.

Noticing Vincenzo's hard stare, Emilia realized her words could be misconstrued as an invitation to spend the night together. "Alone," she blurted. "That wasn't a suggestion or anything." Her cheeks flamed, as she stumbled to clear up the miscommunication.

"Nothing other than paperwork, which I would love to make wait." Semi-disappointed her words weren't intended as a come-on, he felt an undeniable attraction to the complex woman beside him. "I hoped we could discuss what led you to Texas."

"I came for a couple of crucial business meetings, but I hadn't planned for how much emotional headspace being back in Texas would chew up. Last minute, I asked my assistant to chair the important meetings while I took a much-needed reprieve and focused on a passion project instead." Emilia fell silent, overcome by emotion once more, thinking of the widows she would be meeting with as part of the inauguration process of the foundation.

"What will you do here?" He asked the purposefully open-ended question to learn more about the woman beside him.

She pulled a tube of lip gloss from her purse and applied the scented balm before she responded, choosing her words carefully.

"The usual, I suppose. Sightseeing, shopping, sun and surf." Skirting the reason sounded better than trying to describe how five years ago she made a promise to herself to establish the North American Military Widows Foundation in the city where Mason had proposed to her.

As Emilia applied a shine to her pouty, kissable lips, concern crossed Vincenzo's face as something his father used to say came to mind. *Pretty lips, pretty liar.* Vincenzo's thoughts returned to the discussion he'd had with Russ, his company's private investigator he used for both personal and professional inquiries, the last of which had been tracking down his wife who'd run off and disappeared.

Earlier that evening…

"Russ, Vincenzo here," he said as the phone connected, propping his legs atop the desk in front of him. With his mother and Emilia gone for a walk, Vincenzo wasted no time setting the hound on the hunt. His fingers itched for a cigarette—a habit he'd given up several years ago, but missed at times like these. There was something about this woman. He didn't know what yet, but he would find out.

"Thought I might hear from you," Russ said. He began rattling off case details they hadn't spoken of since his last update on either Strazzo's latest antics or Vincenzo's divorce proceedings. There was not much of note, but Vincenzo's focus was elsewhere anyway.

"I have something new for you to look into," Vincenzo said. He laid down the relevant details—Emilia running into his brother at the airport, then the mishap with the shuttle, and the family dinner.

Russ had seen the encounter at the airport firsthand. He'd been there to ensure from the shadows that Strazzo didn't make any unnecessary scenes before his flight. "From where I stood, I saw a woman with a suitcase cut her off. Her heel twisted hard. She fell forward. Strazzo rushed like a gentleman to catch her."

"That's a first." His brother might have one courteous bone in his body, but it was likely the one he used the most to get lucky.

"Agreed," Russ said skeptically. "We both know Strazzo's appetites. He probably did it to make himself look good."

"Yup, probably looking for another fifteen minutes of fame. God, this kid is going be the death of me." Vincenzo's annoyance quickly returned to suspicion. "But this is different. The woman isn't the usual Strazzo shrapnel." He furrowed his brow. "It couldn't all be coincidence. I'm certain she's hiding something."

"I'm on it," Russ said.

Nearly an hour later, Vincenzo made a quick call to Russ for an update before the women returned from their walk.

"It's Vincenzo. I only have a minute or two," he said into the receiver.

"I couldn't find any previous record of contact between Strazzo and this woman," Russ replied, scratching his head for a moment and remembering the pretty brunette who'd entered Strazzo's path.

"Anything you can tell me about her?" Vincenzo twirled a pen in his hand, wishing his gut didn't tell him something was off about the whole situation.

"Bit more detail I can add to your documentation: Emilia Patric, aged thirty-five, lived abroad for several years. Worked in France and Italy. Currently lives in Canada," Russ trotted out in list form. "Oh, and she flew in on a chartered flight—make of that what you will."

Vincenzo put his legs down and leaned in, hunched over. Intrigued by what came next, pen in hand, he captured the particulars of Russ' investigative debrief.

"Flight info is unclear. A numbered company paid for it, but there are several others on the passenger's list. Odd if you ask me," Russ said, looking at the paperwork he'd collected thus far.

"Any idea when they'll return and where it's headed?" Vincenzo prompted, teasing out a bit more of the puzzle.

"Looks like three weeks from now, October fifteenth is the scheduled return," Russ said. "Don't have a return destination yet."

"Same passengers?" Vincenzo wondered if there were any events around town he'd seen advertised that might correspond to her arrival.

"No. The passenger manifest is constantly changing," Russ said.

Looking out the window, Vincenzo saw his mother's car returning. "Okay, let this sit with me for a few, Russ. Maybe I can pry a little and find out what our dear Emilia is up to on this trip." He knew his mother would expect him to drive Emmi back to the hotel later. He'd make small talk then.

"Fine by me. Maybe connect in a week? It might be nothing except what it seems."

"Wouldn't that be nice," Vincenzo said wearily. He was tired of the constant maneuvering by less than scrupulous individuals and Hex Holdings competitors.

"Wouldn't it?" Russ answered before he hung up.

Pulling into Galveston, Vincenzo found the Resort and Conference Center facing the water and drove into the hotel lot across from the Gulf.

With wistful longing, Emmi noted an interracial couple walking by with linked hands. The milkiness of the woman's skin beautifully complemented the dark brown complexion of her husband. The two lovebirds were engrossed in deep conversation. Their tinkling laughter echoed long after they passed. Her gaze shifted from the departing couple to her lap where Vincenzo's hand still held hers.

After parking the car, they made their way into the lobby of their intended destination. "Give me a minute."

"Sure, no problem," he said as she ambled up to the marble front desk. He grabbed a cup of coffee. After booking a room, Vincenzo insisted he was off the clock and didn't mind waiting for her to freshen up.

Taking him up on his offer, Emmi went to her room and kicked her shoes in different directions, only to collect them and place them neatly by the door. Stepping into the shower and feeling the refreshing warmth of the water sluice over her, she recapped the events of the day, wondering what further embarrassment the night would hold.

Emilia Patric, always looking around for the funeral when someone gives you flowers. You're much too cynical.

Finished showering, her formerly straightened hair showed its natural wave as it hung down her back. She changed into a dark denim pair of shorts that hugged her bottom's ample curve, paired with a cotton shirt and a thin cable knit sweater, and went downstairs.

Vincenzo looked up from a newspaper to see her standing over him. His breath catching for a moment, he noticed she'd gone to the trouble of changing and fixing her hair. He could smell the light scent from the shampoo she must have used in the shower, and the flicker of desire he felt fanned. He tread a fine line. Until it became clear who she was or what her intentions were, he needed to remain vigilant. *Who am I kidding?* He was already involved. Otherwise, he wouldn't have been envious of Strazzo.

"Follow me." He took her hand and headed for a section of the city known as The Strand, a tourist trap famous for its nineteenth-century architecture, a castle, and an opera house.

***

Two hours later, they embraced on the floor of the *Lonely Hearts* bar at the hotel, swaying to a slow song. The liquor's effect moderately dulled her senses, leaving behind a relaxed feeling of well-being.

"Vincenzo?" she murmured against his chest, wondering what he'd think of her if she said what was on her mind.

"Yes?" he answered, lost in the sweet fragrance of her hair and the softness of her body. He'd long forgotten about staying on guard. He imagined her hair spread out on her hotel pillow next to him, his lips pressed between the valley of her breasts.

Emmi stammered, preparing herself for his anticipated no. Voicing her thoughts before she lost her courage, she said in a seductive voice, "I want to be with you." Emmi exhaled the last of her breath as she waited for his reply.

"Emilia, I'm not sure what you're asking. I'm not sure *you* know what you're asking." They'd had more than a few drinks.

"Vincenzo," she said, pulling back from him a little to look him in his eyes. "I am a woman who knows what I want. And right now, I want you."

***

Emmi sat opposite him on her hotel bed, the moment weighing heavily on her mind. Mason had taken her virginity. She was suddenly uncertain if she was ready to be this bold after so long. "I'm not on birth control." She nervously rearranged the pillows, plucking imaginary fluff from the covers.

He reached across the tacky bedspread, his fingers grazing her cheek to remove the hair that stuck to her lip, brushing it away before he leaned in to graze her lips with a sweet, light kiss. "It's okay."

Her skin prickled at his touch, just as it had the first time his lips had lingered on her wrist, and during their first kiss in his mother's house. Salacious thoughts she'd kept to herself surfaced once more as she thought of his hair whispering across her thighs.

Vincenzo delicately removed the scarf Mason had given her, along with her pearl necklace, to trace the outline of her collarbone with kisses. As he did so, another jab of desire coursed through her. Continuing his trail of kisses, a distinct whiff of liquor reached his nostrils as she sighed with a tiny moan. As much as he desired her, he hesitated on the button of her jean shorts. *Mia cara.* Disappointed before he'd even uttered the next words, Vincenzo pulled away from her and looked up to the ceiling.

"We can't."

Please Don't Call

Vincenzo woke and looked around the unfamiliar room he was in. His gaze shifted to the figure lying next to him. Remembering the sequence of events from the night prior, he must've fallen asleep in Emmi's hotel room.

He listened to her peaceful breathing as her face lay inches from his. He admired her full lips, remembering the kiss he'd given them hours earlier. Feeling his desire grow, he abruptly looked away only to linger on the silken rise of her hips and round bottom.

He swallowed hard and forced his eyes to read the clock on the table beside her hair, wishing he could run his fingers through its length. The early morning hour glared back at him as he deliberated if he should leave before she woke.

He quietly slipped out of the bed and gathered his belongings, hesitating a moment before deciding to leave her his number. Using the hotel's pen and pad, he scribbled a quick note. His heart pounded as he laid it on the pillow beside her, wondering if she'd call, wondering if he even wanted her to.

He closed the door to her room as quietly as he could, ensuring it was locked behind him, and started down the hall. *Who is this woman? Does she have ill intentions toward me and my family? Will she hurt me the way Isabella had?*

Maybe it would be best if he didn't hear from her after all.

Emilia woke to the sound of a plaintive cry. As an inquisitive seagull perched cheekily on the railing outdoors. The winged menace cocked its head and squawked noisily. Its pink feet trundled along the bar looking for the remnants of an easy meal.

She stretched and rolled over to stare bleary-eyed at the time. Six o'clock, the display read. Her head pulsating from too much wine, she shifted her feet to the floor and padded across the dusky gray rise of carpet toward the closet.

Throwing on the gold-insignia-embossed hotel robe, she wondered if she dared presume the hotel coffee was palatable. Setting the single-serve pot to percolate, she stepped into the steamy shower to start the day.

Ten minutes later, she turned on the morning news and winced as she tasted the coffee, finding it strong enough to stand a fork in. Palatable was a relative term. *How do Americans drink this crap?* She'd give her left ovary for Timmies right now. Maybe even the right one too, if they threw in a maple pecan danish.

She grimaced, taking another sip as she listened to the anchor report on an altercation overseas. Another soldier was killed in the line of duty. Several more were injured in the same area where Mason's body had been found.

The usual gut-punch of the headlines fled quickly, as a gust of warm September wind blew the white gauze of the hotel curtains inward and then back out. The seagull who'd been begging for a free meal lifted off and was carried away by an updraft. She walked out on the balcony and watched as the gull floated effortlessly in the air. Breathing in the brine-tinged air, she listened as the ocean pummeled the darkened sand of the shore.

She was glad Vincenzo had gone. Feeling torn between guilt about being with someone other than Mason and wanting to repeat the previous evening's events, Emilia was relieved that the decision had been made for her. *He's engaged… What have I done?* Finding his number on the hotel pad on her pillow, she tore the paper free, crumpled it up, and tossed it into the trash, seeing no reason other than lust and loneliness to contact him again. Neither were compelling enough reasons to do so.

Deciding to walk along the sand, she took up her purse. Feeling the inner pocket for the keycard. She dumped the contents onto the bed and searched its interior, then moved on to the items on the bed. *Lipstick, wallet, house keys, stamps…* Her eyes widened and her heart rate increased when she realized what was missing—no forest motif print scarf, nor the strand of pearls. A quick swipe of her hand, and all items were back in the bag.

"Oh, no." Emmi's hand covered her gaping mouth as she thought about how he had taken them off of her neck. "Dear lord." *I all but begged him to sleep with me.* Her palms began to moisten. Feeling torn between her still-fresh desire and her complete embarrassment, she fished his number out of the trash, her face scarlet with remembrance.

Vincenzo drove the route from Galveston aggressively. He wasn't the type of man to get involved. Nor the type to chase women. He couldn't recall the last time a woman had dismissed him. Emmi had done so gently, and yet he couldn't help but feel drawn to her, dreaming of wrapping her smooth body in his arms, imagining her full lips on his.

But when he'd stopped them from doing anything they might regret, Emmi had spoken of things he wasn't ready to hear. He blinked the tears from his eyes as he recalled their conversation from the night prior.

Snuggled into his chest, Emmi let the alcohol spill all her deepest secrets. "Five years ago, I built a small room off our bedroom for when my husband was scheduled to return. What could be the harm in that? We'd decided to start a family. Mason was at the end of his tour.

"I want a little boy with brown eyes," she continued, closing her own eyes to envision her imaginary children. "I can see his little sister too. Her hair is lighter. Maybe she has his eyes and my nose. The poor thing has my nose," Emilia cried out in drunken dismay.

Vincenzo's throat tightened as he continued driving toward home. He'd had similar dreams. At least, until Isabella had disappeared. How long had he searched for her now? Mercurial creatures, women were. Most thought him handsome, some thought his accent sexy. The rest were after his money.

Emilia, though—the image of her face popping into his mind—he was sure she wanted him. Passion and desire were in her touch, she had a softness about her. He trusted her—or at least he wanted to. If she hadn't dismissed him, he'd have turned around and tried to change her mind.

"I won't ask you to call me. There isn't a day I don't recollect when they brought him home in a casket. Every day is that day." She paused momentarily before continuing. "I've been on my own for five years, hit success goals I never envisioned. It's garbage, Vincenzo. Worthless, without him. Nothing will ever be the same again."

As the liquor wore off, her words touched a hollow part of him. The days he'd lay alone drinking whiskey in his empty apartment, staring at the garbage collecting around him—the takeout wrappers as ripe as the excuses he told himself for continuing that way.

He tried to comfort her. "Your life paused, Emmi." He stroked her shoulder as they lay together. His arms around her, her legs entwined with his. He repeated words his mother had said to him after she'd shown up at his door several months into his depression after his wife left.

Finding him drunk and unshaven, Vitoria instructed him, "Vincenzo, shave, shower, get up. You grieve, but the chasm of emptiness you feel today will overflow with joy tomorrow because *the wound is so deep today." He remembered the impact his mother's words had on him. He hoped they reached Emmi's heart and comforted her, just as they had done for him.*

Emilia and Vincenzo were both vulnerable, both hurt from relationships that no longer existed. In that moment, they had reached out and found each other. Vincenzo remembered vividly what had happened next between them. Emilia had stared deep into his eyes, lips slightly parted but no words leaving them. He was sure his heart had stopped for a second before she leaned in and kissed him. Unable to resist her a second time, their bodies met with a fiery passion that could not be quenched.

Vincenzo didn't believe in love at first sight, but he couldn't shake the protective emotions Emmi elicited from him, telling himself it was just the time they'd shared that made him feel more than he had in years. As Vincenzo continued his journey back to Houston, he couldn't deny that he wanted more, and that terrified him.

His phone rang, interrupting his thoughts. An unknown number flashed across the screen. "Vincenzo Eton," he answered, suspecting it was one of the companies he'd reached out to earlier. The extended delay on the line caused him to look at his phone, wondering if he crossed a dead spot in cell coverage. "Hello?" he repeated.

"Vincenzo," a voice said finally. "It's Emilia. Any chance you have a strand of freshwater pearls somewhere on your person? And a silk scarf?"

Muttering something that sounded like profanity under his breath, Vincenzo patted his coat pocket, feeling something inside.

"Excuse me?"

Taking a deep breath, he said, "They're here." Recollecting how he had taken the scarf off her neck, he thought of how it had interfered with the pathway from her nape to her breast. His thoughts trailed off to how his fingers had felt on her silken skin.

He shook his head to clear his thoughts, remembering he hadn't listened to the message Russ had left in his voicemail. It'd have to wait until after his meeting. He was running late.

"Oh, thank god. Would it be too much to ask you to leave them at the hotel in Houston? I'm scheduled to check in there a few days from now." Her heart and mind whispered in tandem the advice she didn't want to hear.

"I'm in a board meeting at ten. I could see you after. When are you checking out of your hotel in Galveston?" Vincenzo asked, doing a rough calculation of the time it would take him to attend the meeting and return.

"I hadn't decided, I was thinking I would stay another night. Enjoy some of the nightlife," she said, the plans solidifying in her head as she spoke. *Ask him to join you tonight.*

"We didn't get to see all the places I promised last night." His voice shifted to a warm and suggestive timbre. "We could make another night of it…" He trailed off, allowing her time to think it through.

Emmi's thoughts went to the way his hands had touched her shoulders as they danced.

The kisses they'd shared. Her mind mentally filling in the blanks of what would naturally come next. She loved a calculated risk, but affairs of the heart were never not messy. She was a serial monogamist. Nor was she about to start a relationship simply because she was lonely.

"Emilia, are you still there?" he asked, thinking the signal had dropped again.

"Yes, I'm here." She hesitated, replying against her better judgment. "When do you think you'll get here?"

"I'll be there at six." He waited until she hung up. His heart thudding a little faster. Leaning in, he cranked the tune that played softly across his speakers and as he neared Houston.

Sitting on the hotel bed, she rose to grab paper and pen. After learning Vincenzo's last name, a small fragment of the puzzle slipped into place. Recollecting the change in his demeanor the evening before and the level of viciousness when he'd interrogated her at dinner, it had felt like she was missing something.

Eton. Eye-tun, Vincenzo had pronounced it on the phone. Where have I heard that name before?

Opening a browser tab on her phone, Emmi queried several keywords, finding everything from exquisitely tailored shirts to high-end automotive parts. The shirts seemed to fit the profile of the man who drove an electric car, had expensive taste in suits, and sang along to old songs when he thought no one was listening. Nothing further though to link him to the name.

Maybe I'll have better luck in the image search.

The first page of images yielded nothing of interest. On the second page, a single small black-and-white photo of Vincenzo and Strazzo from a newspaper clipping caught her eye. "The Eton Brothers: How Postgraduate Degrees in

Philosophy, and Politics and Economics Turned the World of Technology Upside Down."

Emilia's eyes scanned the page to see if there was any connection to her business endeavors. "The cagey son of a whoremonger." Her gaze locked on the name of Vincenzo's company. If arbitrations had been ugly before, things were going to get positively nasty. Picking up her phone again, she fired off a rapid message to Danny, and called him a few minutes later.

"You're on vacation, boss lady," Danny said.

"Have you sent off the paperwork for Hex Holdings?" Emmi asked, visualizing the mountain of paperwork he was sifting through. Despite what appeared a lack of organization, Danny's desk was under a pile of carefully placed papers. He'd never lost a contract, nor dropped a project in the four years he'd worked for her.

"Good morning to you too, Emmi. Actually, no," he said. "Our guy in corporate law stopped by. He asked me to make four copies for the ten o'clock meeting this morning. Was there something you needed?"

"Kiss Donald's bald little head for me," Emilia said in pleasant spirits. "I need you to encrypt a copy and send it to me. I'm at a hotel in Galveston. I'll be sitting in on the video conference after I make a phone call. Maybe we can get this done today."

"Why? Have magical fairies come and sprinkled arbitration dust? Or unicorns. Maybe some rainbow-horned unicorns. You haven't been smoking the Houston herb have you, Emilia Patric?"

"Is that any kind of question to ask a boss on her holidays? I swear Danny, I would smack you if I were there," Emmi said.

"If you are, I need pictures," he quipped almost predictably. "Maybe I could sell them to supplement the paltry salary you give me."

"Ugh, why I keep you is beyond me." Emilia sighed with forced emphasis. "Send me the document so I don't have to drive there and abuse you with my stiletto."

"It's because I'm pretty, isn't it?" Danny remarked with pouty emphasis.

"What have I told you about profanity in the office?" Emmi wrinkled her nose at his use of a reference to beauty, sitting on the hotel bed with a smile on her face. If she had to hazard a guess, he was dressed to the nines as usual. The off-red suit jacket with the checkered bowtie. With a dark slack. He probably was looking quite stylish.

"Excuse me, the jar has both our names on it. After raiding it to buy cookies from the club, which shall remain nameless, and almonds for Cheryl's kid in accounting, you're still a hundred bucks ahead of me, potty-mouth Patric!" He paused, before declaring enthusiastically, "There, sent."

"Thank you. Talk later, and behave," Emilia chided, realizing Danny's spitfire character and sarcasm were the highlights of her days.

Vincenzo strode into the boardroom and began setting up. As his laptop screen's background substituted the presentation board's deep blue, he worked the room, ensuring he made a point of shaking hands with those he hadn't met.

Seeing refreshments on a table alongside the wall, he poured himself a glass of water from a crystal carafe as his phone buzzed, reminding him to silence the unit. Emilia's number flickered across it. Checking his watch, he considered not answering. Though, if she'd changed her mind about dinner, he didn't want her to weasel out via voicemail.

"Hello, Emilia. We're about to begin the session I mentioned. Speak fast, please," Vincenzo answered in a clipped, but pleasant voice.

Hesitant to broach the subject, Emilia opted for the fewest words. "Your meeting is with my team, Vincenzo." A pregnant pause dilated and filled the airwaves between them. "I didn't know. Until you mentioned your last name on the phone earlier."

"What exactly do you mean by your team? Do you head up research and development at OPV?" His assumption gave off a chilly tone.

Emmi's heart took a nosedive, uneasy to discover his opinion of her capability of success mattered so much to her. "Not exactly."

"Emilia, we can discuss this tonight. I don't have time for this right now. I'm sorry. I need to hang up now," he said, glancing at his watch and wondering when the CEO of OPV was intending to show.

Vincenzo froze as a connection clicked in his thoughts. *No. It couldn't be.* He'd received a last-minute text stating the company owner of OPV would be making an appearance in the meeting mere minutes before Emilia had called. *Could the timing between the text and her call just be coincidence?* Emmi didn't have the waspish demeanor that made men quake like some female CEOs he'd met. Either way, he needed to concentrate and bring his A-game.

Vincenzo took his seat at the table as the boardroom of the Galveston hotel came into view on the screen. Shocked from instant recognition of the face on the screen in front of him, Vincenzo hardly noticed as Danny began speaking to his right.

"Good morning, everyone. Since there are new faces around the table, I'll start with an introduction. As most of you know, I'm Danny Davinski. I'll be leading the meeting this morning. Joining us virtually from Galveston is Mrs. Emilia

Patric, owner and CEO of OPV Enterprises. Mrs. Patric is away on vacation this week, but wanted to keep abreast of progress in the third quarter."

Vincenzo glared at the viewscreen. He couldn't believe he hadn't realized who she was until now. OPV Enterprises had a firm grasp on Hex Holdings ever since his father had been alive. Could she have been lying to him this whole time? Did she really know who he was all along?

Selling similar product lines, Vincenzo's company had been forced to approach hers and ask for financial backing in exchange for company shares, putting them firmly in OPV Enterprises' debt.

Ever since, the Eton family no longer had the final say in what their company did. Now, they had to consult with her company for every little detail, along with these damn quarterly reports. He was sick and tired of feeling controlled by someone who didn't know how hard it had been for his grandfather to get this company off the ground. To top it off, he believed the stress of being under someone else's thumb had accelerated his father's poor health, and he blamed her company for his untimely loss.

Clueless to the connection and building tension, Danny continued with the meeting. "First up, we have Vincenzo Eton, Hex Holdings CEO, accompanied by VP Ulric with third-quarter reporting. Whenever you're ready, gentlemen."

Vincenzo shook off the betrayal he felt, and walked through projections for the upcoming quarter, each piece supporting why Hex Holdings needed to remain independent rather than merging with OPV.

"Comments, or questions?" Vincenzo asked, opening it up to the floor. With the presentation complete, the comments volleyed from both sides. Avoiding Emilia's gaze, he answered the questions Danny posed, Vincenzo's voice rising with angry emotion each time he spoke.

Finally, Emmi called for attention above the din. "I'm hearing a lot of murmuring about access to the product. If the kit needs to be free for a time to catch consumers who fall through the cracks, we'll eat the cost."

"That's suicide. You'll run both companies into the ground," Vincenzo interjected.

"Hardly. I've spoken with a few angel investors, lined up some venture capitalists. They're ready to align their name with ours. If you'd like, we can take this offline and discuss it. The offer still stands, Vincenzo."

"Sidebar conversations won't address the fact that my family has invested three generations to this product line. Are you so blinded by corporate consumerism that you don't see how Hex Holdings represents something beyond a product?"

"Are you so traditional you'd let the company line die instead of agreeing to the merger? Don't you see that one is superior to none?" Emilia asked pointedly, her own emotions joining in now.

"Yes. I'm also traditional enough to appreciate that you don't screw your way into a takeover," he countered, looking at her as though she were a fragment of gum stuck to his shoe.

Emilia shifted in her seat to sit up straight, shoulders squared, staring him down through virtual space. "Funny thing, Vincenzo. I didn't hear a peep of protest from you when we were in bed last night."

Danny's gasp filled the space, his face swiveled to look at Emilia with barely contained joy.

"Go to hell." Vincenzo's barely contained rage echoed in the slam of the door against the wall as he walked out of the boardroom.

Too little, too late, Vincenzo thought angrily as he got off the phone. Having stormed out of the boardroom, Vincenzo had taken the opportunity to call Russ back, who had discovered the connection between Hex Holdings and Emilia. Thinking how Russ had so far failed to find Isabella, and now to warn him of this connection, Vincenzo wondered why he even bothered to pay the PI's retainer.

The Hex Holdings VP cleared his throat. "Um, just give me a minute, please." At Emmi's nod, Ulric stood and disappeared off-screen.

Seeing Emilia shift uncomfortably, Danny pulled out his phone and shot off a text.

"Oh my god. This is huge. How did you hook up with him? Nice move on the power pantsuit, by the way. You're looking bossilicious over there."

Emilia looked down at her phone when it pinged and picked it up, grateful for the distraction.

"Why, thank you. I could only be hotter if I were brandishing a flamethrower with slicked back hair in a Robert Palmer video. As for Vincenzo, I didn't know. I got into the wrong vehicle, ended up at his mother's house, and things went from there."

Danny chuckled gleefully as he typed out a response and hit send. *"Dear god. Don't tell me you shagged the CEO of Hex at his mother's house."*

Emilia glared at him through their screens. Her middle finger extended as she grasped her cup, a silent gesture only he would interpret.

Danny kept texting. *"All kidding aside, do you need a dramatic rescue?"*

"Maybe, but if this is going to be some epic scene, I need to prepare for it. I need details."

"So, I was envisioning I'd call and say I was your second cousin, twice removed, who was married to your sister's brother's baby daddy, Linda Sue."

"That name doesn't sound made up at all. But, by all means, do go on."

"I'd wail and moan. Then have a complete meltdown about seeing my man out with another woman. Still following me?"

"I'm invested, but where do you plan on finding rednecks? I need to know where the rednecks are coming from."

"Oh, ye of little faith. I only need to call my sister's cousin's mother, and it's done. Say the word, and it's drama town, potty mouth Patric."

Emilia shook her head at Danny's ridiculousness and set her phone down. She began to clear the items in front of her without a word, assuming the meeting was about to officially end.

Ulric came back on screen without Vincenzo. The threat of company closure notwithstanding, Ulric found Emilia's suggestions to be a definitive step up from where they'd been several months ago, and he told her as much. While he was certain Vincenzo needed to address what happened between himself and the head of OPV Enterprises, it was clear Vincenzo had lost focus on how this deal would make their product a household name. What's more, it fulfilled the visionary goal Vincenzo's father, Benedict, had for it when he was still alive.

"No one wants to ask the question, but I will. If we agree to merge, how many staff will you lay off, rather than your firm just owning the lion's share of our stocks?" Ulric asked, picking up his phone, ready to crunch the numbers.

She opened her mouth to answer when Vincenzo reentered the room. His face remained taut with anger as he listened to Ulric and Emilia talk shop, waiting for what he knew was to come. He'd done it a hundred times before. Mergers always meant substantial layoffs.

Having anticipated the question, Emilia responded with a positive that surprised both Hex Holdings men. "We need experienced personnel to run the company, with buyouts for those we want to retire. Preliminary numbers suggest we'll retain close to eighty-five percent."

Vincenzo interjected. Even with such a great number, his eyes were marked with resentment. "There's no dead weight here, Emilia."

"Presumably not, but there are employees who rack up unnecessary business lunches and plane tickets to France, others months away from retiring. You may be blinded by familial connections, but I am not," Emilia remarked, both of them knowing she was alluding to Strazzo, who hadn't bothered to attend despite missing his flight.

Vincenzo complained, "My brother's expenditures are none of your business." Enraged at her thinly veiled threat, knowing his brother was likely part of the fifteen percent to be sacked.

"No, but it is the board of directors business, of which I chair. It would be advisable for Strazzo's long-term interest to slug it out in the trenches instead of relying on the generosity of his brother's wallet and solid business reputation."

"A rising tide lifts all boats, Mrs. Patric."

"Not when there is a hole in their hull, Mr. Eton."

With Emilia's last word on the matter, Danny quickly grabbed the reins once more and closed the meeting while the board remained hopeful for a solution.

"Vincenzo, would you stay behind so we could discuss…?" Emilia asked, eager to offer an olive branch, uncomfortable with the way things had ended between them.

"No. Fire me if you like." Turning toward the sound of a door opening, he added, "I need to cancel our previous supper arrangement." Emilia watched as her doppelganger crossed the room and kissed Vincenzo on the cheek.

"Ready?" Sondra asked Vincenzo. Then, noticing Emilia on the screen, "Oh, hi! Sorry, but I must take this man away from you now."

Away from me, indeed. Imagining that they were off to work on wedding plans, Emilia waved at her and tried to repress all of the emotions that washed over her like waves—despondence, guilt, anger. "Hi, Sondra." Quelling her disappointment, she shuffled the pages in front of her and addressed Vincenzo again. "I'll have my team take the lead on matters, just as we have been doing for the past eight months."

Strazzo flipped through channels in the basement of his mother's manor, his feet up on the coffee table in front of the television. Nothing on except mindless trash and infomercials, his sense of ennui increased as he thought of his last conversation with Sondra.

"You must be joking, right? Date you? You've got no direction. You're always chasing after some skirt. Go on, pull the other leg."

Her words had hurt. Her laughter had hurt even more. She'd dismissed his vulnerability and he hadn't heard from her since. Strazzo thought about how all his actions of late distanced himself from his father's mold. While his father valued structure and rule-based reasoning, Strazzo believed if it felt right, there was no reason he shouldn't follow wherever it led.

Except it *didn't* feel right this time.

He didn't know how he'd missed it during all these years of friendship with her, but his eyes were finally opened—Sondra was the one for him. But something had changed since she'd joked about the diamond ring over two months ago. She'd grown distant, guarded. She used to call *him*. Now she ignored his calls. The only comfort he found was in the bottle, but the more alcohol he consumed, the less peace of mind he had. His actions left him feeling hollow.

Lost in his thoughts, Strazzo's eyes suddenly focused on the current commercial. It was a financial appeal for Physicians Abroad. Refugees in boats, young men such as himself, who should be in the prime of their life, thin as his cousin when he was twelve. Their brilliant white teeth crooked, some broken, while his own ran straight. He knew the commercial aimed to obtain a visceral response from those who watched it—their agenda to nudge donors in the right direction, to open their wallets, and give generously. As they should.

Irrespective of the appeal, mixed feelings of guilt and regret arose in him. He had goals before all of this. With his father's death, he found himself suddenly pressed into the family business, and now he felt trapped. How could he abandon his family for his selfish desires?

Shutting off the enormous television in front of him, he still visualized the commercial. A medical clinic's shanty style with the bare necessities required to treat the patients who came through the door. It was the children who disturbed him the most. He knew it wasn't a sin to be rich, but he felt the weight of his behavior. All the stupid things he had done came to roost in his mind. Doing nothing was a crime when even a small gesture could do much good.

Slapping his gut, Strazzo walked into his room, peeled a clean shirt off the hanger, and slipped it on. Grabbing his cell from the desk in his room, he clicked on the university's webpage and navigated the links he'd saved on his phone from three years ago before his father's death. Determined to act before he talked himself out of it, he seized his motorcycle helmet from the closet and put on his leather jacket. Vincenzo wasn't going to like his plan one bit, but he didn't care.

The registrar's office was in chaos when Strazzo arrived. A petite and frazzled middle-aged woman handled the incoming calls on her continuously flashing switchboard with efficient aplomb.

"I will be with you in a minute, sir." Papers in hand, she walked briskly into an adjoining office.

Strazzo took a glance at the faces of the youth around him. One smiled in recognition, while the other three remained oblivious.

Returning to her station, the clerk asked, "How may I assist you?"

"I'd like to apply to medical school," he replied.

"Have you started your application online?" she queried. Her tone ripe with agitation, having been asked the same question by at least forty-five other budding doctors who had about as much possibility of becoming medical professionals as she did becoming dean.

"Yes, but I graduated four years ago. There have been some changes since," Strazzo added quickly, sensing the woman would gleefully bludgeon him with the nearest phone book if he weren't specific.

"You'll need to make an appointment to see our career advisor. We don't have time for walk-ins today," the secretary said, ready to touch her headset and answer the phone as it started ringing again.

"I don't think you appreciate the situation, Miss…Burnett," Strazzo said, reading the woman's last name from her nameplate on her desk.

"I'm certain I do. Your lack of planning doesn't constitute an emergency on my part. As you can see, there are four individuals with appointments in the waiting area." She gestured to the cramped room.

A slender youth with a man bun sat to the furthest right, flanked by a cheeky-looking woman in a pair of black horn-rimmed glasses. With a seat between them, a bucktoothed, tawny-haired youth whose face was covered in pimples sat playing some strategy game on his phone, taking a break to nod at Strazzo. The last, a studious girl who sat organizing her papers, which already appeared to be organized, collated, and tagged with a variety of colorful notes.

"Surely you can squeeze one more in," Strazzo pressed.

The clerk looked at him with contempt. "I don't know who you imagine you are, but this is not the way we do things here. You'll need to make an appointment like everyone else." Her demeanor gave him the impression that even if he'd been the president of the United States, she'd have made him wait if he hadn't had the sense to book in advance.

Clearing his throat, he addressed the quartet who sat in the uncomfortable chairs around the room. "If I paid for your tuition, would you let me take your appointment?" The words *paid tuition* motivated their immediate consideration. Waking from their phone comas, one was amused, the other three doubtful. Curious to see if he really would—or even could—pay off their enormous debt, they remained silent, ready for whatever came next.

He reached into his pocket and grabbed a receipt from earlier. "How much do you have left to pay? Specifically, for the rest of your program."

The students answered in turn—thirty thousand, seventy-five thousand, fifty thousand, and a hundred thousand.

"May I borrow a pen?" Strazzo asked. Retrieving a half-chewed pencil from one of the youths, he did a back-of-the-envelope calculation. "So, two hundred and fifty-five thousand total."

"Yep," confirmed the lanky, pimple-completed young man. The studious one stared, her gaze boring through him. Man-Bun looked ready to Instagram something.

"Ms. B. here will schedule you another meeting?" He looked questioningly between the amazed students and the overwhelmed clerk.

"Fine by me," said the keener. "You had me at free tuition."

"Heck, yeah!" the second said, doing some sort of hand-wavy, fist-pump action like she was having a seizure—probably jacked up on cosplay and anime, judging by her manga-inspired T-shirt.

"Thank you so much," said the third in a shy, quiet voice, thinking he'd rather be at home coding anyhow.

"I'm going to faint," the last girl said, fanning herself with her hands.

Strazzo looked at her face. She *was* pale. "Put your head between your knees." He pulled up a chair, sitting in front of her.

"One hundred thousand dollars? Man, I came here to withdraw from my program, I couldn't afford to continue. I've been eating noodles for weeks now." The girl started to ugly cry.

Strazzo said nothing as each of them spoke of how difficult it had been to get through each month. From the stress of studying, trying to navigate the financial assistance supports, to being hugely indebted to parents who were barely making ends meet themselves.

"My mom remortgaged her house so I could come," Noodle Girl sobbed, bawling harder. The rest of them gathered around her, unable to believe their good fortune.

Strazzo was deeply moved. He hadn't given any consideration to how fortunate he was to have parents footing the bill for everything.

Turning back to Ms. B., Strazzo looked at her until she squirmed in her office chair. Her gaze darted from side to side looking as if she might soon have an aneurysm of some sort.

"It would seem an opening has arisen. Be a peach and pencil me in?" He smiled sweetly at her.

Not missing a beat, the clerk collected herself. "Will that be a cashier's check or credit card?"

"Centurion." He pulled the slim black card from his worn leather wallet—one of the last presents and mementos he carried around from his father. The secretary's face blanched as she saw the name on the card.

"Didn't know who I was, did you?"

With a self-indulgent sniff, she rang up the totals and took the student's names out of the book she kept in front of her. She handed each of the students a paid receipt, and printed off one for Strazzo as well. "Tax purposes, of course. One act of charity deserves another." Ms. B. smiled at him for the first time, her afternoon cleared for the day.

"Of course." *Should have retired the old bat instead. Would have helped the kids more.*

"Oh, Dot, was it?" Gleaning the students' names from the receipt, Strazzo addressed Noodle Girl as he dug into his wallet. Retrieving a couple of crisp hundos, he stretched his hand toward her. "You won't go hungry today. I've got you covered."

"I couldn't. You've done more than enough."

"Not a word of this to anyone you hear?" Strazzo said as he pushed the money into her palm. "I have a rich playboy image to live up to the ladies' love," he said, pew-pewing with a couple of cheesy finger guns. He wondered how many of his previous schoolmates had gone hungry so they could keep getting an education. He made a mental note to ask Vincenzo to set up a trust fund for struggling students.

Watching the students walk out of the registrars to get the nicest meal they'd had in a long time as they discussed their fortune for being in the right place at the right time, Strazzo turned back to the clerk and slapped the counter. "Time is money. Chop, chop."

Picking up her phone, Ms. B. called the career counselor. "I have a project for you. He has a complex career question he needs to discuss with you."

"Send him in," the counselor said, putting her foot back into the pinchy high heel she wore. Straightening her desk, she pasted a smile on her face and hoped the next session wouldn't take more than an hour.

"Strazzo!?"

"Lisaine Petersen." Genuinely pleased to see his old freshman roommate behind the desk, Strazzo's smile spread across his face. She'd retained her elfin face and tiny figure, still in his mind's eye the twenty-year-old he'd stolen a kiss from. He hadn't regretted much in life, but after lip locking her, their friendship was never the same.

"Lis Frank, now." She rose from behind her desk to grab him in a familiar bear hug.

"You're looking fine. Fine as hell, Lis. Still can't believe Frank finally grew a pair and asked you out."

Lis sighed, eyes shining with genuine happiness, which carried into her voice. "We've been together six years. He's more than I ever imagined." Her infectious smile reached green eyes that matched the emerald on her finger.

"Can't tell you how happy I am for the two of you," Strazzo said, feeling a tiny twinge of regret. Was it for what could've been, or just that he felt like everyone was growing up without him?

"Thank you. Now, where were we?" Lis pulled her chair forward, her thoughts on the transferrable skills which would apply to the degree he was seeking.

Strazzo pulled out his cell phone and passed it to her. "This is what I had in mind."

Lis's eyes sparkled. "Well, you've come to the right place. Let's handle the first part of your plan. I'll check what credits we can transfer to the new degree," she said. She typed away at the computer for a minute or so as she analyzed his grade point average from his previous years at their alma mater.

"Hmm," she said cryptically, turning the computer viewscreen toward him. Several courses hadn't been applied to any specific major. "Any chance you had this degree in mind when you began your previous one?"

"Sort of. After my father passed away, my mother took charge of the business. I needed to be there for her, so I put everything off. After Vincenzo took control of the company, though…" Strazzo trailed off before he said something he'd regret.

A sad look crossed Lis's face. "It was a dark time for you all. I remember worrying you might do something drastic." Relieved to see a changed man in front of her, Lis thought of the times she answered his calls when he had drunk dialed her, eventually changing her number to stop the calls from coming.

Strazzo looked uncomfortable, not willing to plumb the depths of his emotions in her office. Seeing his obvious discomfort, Lis changed the subject. "Here's a list of the remaining classes you need to take. I've enrolled you in as many of the relevant online courses as we have. You can start right away on those. You'll have to attend the labs and lectures, though. They start in the fall. Does that work for you?"

"Yes, but still kind of fuzzy about what to do after that."

Lis laughed. "Not to worry. Come back around after the first semester. We can go over your next steps then. It's not like you have to have everything figured out right now, silly," she said, chiding him as she filed his paperwork in the drawer behind her. "Now, any questions other than what you're going to do for the rest of your life?"

"Any advice on how to break the news to the ever-inflexible Vincenzo? Someone's going to need to talk my brother off a ledge."

"Sorry. You're on your own there, buddy. May as well ask about world peace. What else is going on in your life, are you seeing anyone special?"

Strazzo got a strangled look on his face, an image of Sondra immediately forming in his mind. He couldn't hide a dang thing from Lis in the past, and even less in the present, it seemed.

"Oh, man," Lis said in recognition. "You got it bad. Hot damn, Strazzo's been bagged. Who's the big-game hunter?"

"It's not like that." He tried to deny it, but even he knew he was falling.

A handful of students gawked as Strazzo entered the university bookstore. Others snapped photos as he searched for his texts and incidentals. His eyes landed on a black hoodie emblazoned with the university logo. Grabbing it off the rack, he headed for the checkout.

Dropping the merchandise in front of the round-faced cashier, he looked around while she rang his items through with a starstruck look pasted on her face.

"That'll be seven hundred and fifty-five dollars and thirty-two cents, please."

"Make it an even eight hundred, and give the next student the credit toward their books." He pulled out his wallet and handed her his card. Having done suitable damage to his credit card in the last few hours, he called it a successful day. Exiting the store laden with books, he cursed his lack of forethought as he humped his heavy purchases across the expanse of grounds toward his car.

The campus was beautiful this time of year, with its brick buildings and green spaces. University girls in their late teens and early twenties sunned themselves while buried in homework. Some held hands with their partners, embracing passionately, not caring who looked on. Two handsome twenty-somethings sloughed off the cares of a stressful course load by tossing a frisbee.

As he looked around, he felt a warm sense of belonging and familiarity creep in. Nothing had changed in the four years since he'd been there. He could almost see his younger self tucked into a quiet corner in a study cubicle, headphones in as he hammered out an assignment.

He reached the parking lot two hours late for his parking stub. A willowy redhead with her hair tied back in a severe ponytail stood by his vehicle. Her focus on the ticket pad she wrote on, she noticed him approach and wait for her to finish. Surprised at his silence, the woman side-eyed him, her brown eyes seemingly daring him to show some bravado before recognition struck her.

"Mr. Eton?"

"Yes?"

"You've been here two hours more than your stub allots," she said apologetically, handing him the slip. "Thanks for being a gentleman about it."

"Is that all?" He was surprised she hadn't tried to milk him for a reward to cancel the ticket.

"If you feel you were treated improperly or would like to file a complaint, the number is on the bottom." She moved on to the next car.

Getting into his vehicle, Strazzo stuffed the ticket into his glove box along with the other ten he had accrued, not intending to pay any of them. He used his Bluetooth to connect his phone's music app and turned the volume up. The shred of a guitar blared out of his car as he backed up.

A large man with a gut and an angry countenance caught Strazzo's eye in his rearview mirror. The man's fists were clenched, his face screwed into a mask of rage as he walked purposefully toward the meter maid. Strazzo kept his car at a standstill, watching to see what unfolded.

Reaching the redhead, the fat man started screaming obscenities, making a scene as he grabbed the officer's ticket book and threw it to the ground. She took a step back, clearly on guard as she recognized the man in front of her. The situation escalated quickly as the man lunged forward and proceeded to grab a fistful of her hair, his fist connecting with her lip.

Throwing on the e-brake, Strazzo sprung from behind the wheel. He reached the slack-witted slob who was continuing to pummel the woman, and gripped the man's shoulder firmly.

The guy turned toward him. A sneer of scorn plastered on his enraged face as he saw Strazzo's younger, more attractive looks. Assuming Strazzo was somehow involved with his victim, jealousy overtook the man. "Whatcha gonna do about it, pretty boy?"

"I'm gonna rearrange your face." Strazzo stepped back as the man swung a haymaker, the blow well wide of any possibility of striking him. Strazzo nimbly stepped back in and cracked the man in the face twice—first in the jaw, while the second rearranged the man's nose. Physics was not the fat man's friend that day.

Strazzo gripped his arm, flipped him to his stomach, and pressed his knee forward into the man's back. With his nose bloodied and broken, the man continued to struggle and hurl abusive language. Strazzo controlled the man by applying pressure across the shoulder blade and pressing the man's thumb upward and inward.

"This isn't over, Molly! You can't just walk away from me—you're my wife! You either come home right now, or I'll kill you," the fat man spat out the words, ironic since Strazzo still had physical control of him.

"*Ex*-wife!" the meter maid corrected firmly. "Stop harassing me or we're gonna have a serious problem."

"Are you okay?" Strazzo asked, seeing Molly's facade of bravery fade. She blanched, reliving the trauma as her piece-of-garbage ex-husband struggled under Strazzo's knee. Although it was clear their relationship was volatile, it seemed this was the first time he'd threatened to kill her.

"I have a restraining order against him. This is the second time he's shown up at my place of employment," she said, embarrassed as if somehow her ex-husband's erratic behavior were her fault. She then nodded as if recollecting his earlier question. "Yes, I'm okay." Her eyes remained vacant until Strazzo instructed her to call the police. Visibly shaken, she dialed their number.

The police arrived fifteen minutes later to take Molly's statement, her visibly subdued ex still held by Strazzo. Several bystanders stopped to watch the altercation unfold, while one covertly broadcasted as Houston's Hottie beat a man to a pulp over the honor of a lady.

Of All the Irresponsible, Responsible Things to Do

"Strazzo, you damned fool." Vincenzo hurled his phone at the wall as a reporter from a local news channel reported live from the scene. He'd received a text from Russ with a link to the footage. The action was over, but they kept replaying it from a bystander's cell phone recording. *What is Strazzo even doing there?* Vincenzo paced his home office, rubbing the back of his neck. *Probably trying to pick up some young college girl.*

He drew his left leg across his right knee and settled in the black high-back leather chair in front of his sparsely decorated desk. His gaze sweeping around him, he barely noticed a once-flourishing plant had died in a corner, while a cactus bloomed on a shelving unit, its bulbous body accustomed to long periods of drought. A dusty television lay dormant as he searched for the remote in the drawer. His initial burst of anger dissipated only to rise anew as he considered the numerous instances he and the company investigator had prevented his brother from exposing Hex Holdings to in the last two years alone.

Their father not four days in the grave, rather than go to Spain, Strazzo ordered six bulls and set them loose. Then he proceeded to invite a select few to participate in his version of the running of the bulls just as their father had in his early twenties. While grief did strange things to people, the symbolic send-off became a legal nightmare when one of the servants stepped into the path of the cattle.

Then came Strazzo's "All Nude After Nine." Their otherwise liberal mother came home to find thirty naked men and women in her pool. That in itself was enough to upset her. However, upon retiring for the evening, she entered her bedroom to find one of Strazzo's friends entertaining another in her red lace widow maker. The very same had been pressed in a special box and stored in a safe space in her closet. All the neatly collated love letters she had ever received from her late husband lay carelessly in disarray on her floor.

Vincenzo couldn't recall a time he'd seen her so angry as that. His lips twitched with mirth as he recollected Strazzo's friend's terrified scream. The five-foot-one firecracker had chased the lingerie-wearing man around the room, whipping him with a fine serpentine belt. With a wrath ordinarily associated with the gods, his genteel mother cursed out the offender and all his descendants with a vulgar and highly specific tirade.

She had been inches away from disinheriting Strazzo, threatening him with military school as she had done with another of her sons, when Vincenzo intervened. He shouldn't have. He wasn't a vain man, but he was confident he'd aged five years in the last year alone as he fought to prevent Strazzo from imploding.

He knew the board would call about this latest escapade and he'd better be prepared. They wouldn't tolerate any whiff of violence involving a business partner, no matter how well-intended. On cue, the telephone emitted its familiar jangle as it rang on his desk.

Hex Holdings' vice president was on the line. "Hello, Ulric. You're calling about Strazzo, I presume." Vincenzo cut to the chase, already aggravated he'd soon be eating humble pie concerning Emilia Patric, who rightly called Strazzo a liability after knowing him less than a full day.

"It's all over the news, Vincenzo. We've made a statement condemning his actions. We're capitalizing on public relations by supporting women's shelters in the area."

"We've ridden out worse scandals," Vincenzo replied wearily.

Ulric sighed on the other end before presenting the cold, hard truth. "We're not riding this one out. Strazzo is finished. The board will not allow his conduct to tank the forthcoming merger we have in the hopper."

"I understand," Vincenzo took a deep breath. "I'll fire him myself." Knowing Ulric was right, Vincenzo sat at his desk for a considerable amount of time after hanging up. His own words echoing in his mind.

He thought of how their father would have railed at his brother's conduct and somehow found him to blame for it, rather than the actual culprit. For Benedict Eton, appearances were everything. Perhaps it was too much pressure for Strazzo. If their father had still been alive, he'd have stripped both of them from their positions on the board for this incident, and he would have done it before the end of the live broadcast.

Maybe it was a good thing Pops wasn't around to see what had become of the company his father had built from the ground up.

Picking up the telephone once more, his fingers hovered over the number pad before finally dialing. "Sondra, Vincenzo here." His voice carried a grave tone. "I'm not certain you've seen the news, but I'm getting numerous calls regarding Strazzo."

"I have. I have a news alert that pings every time the Eton name is mentioned."

"Smart. Then you know I'll be fielding calls most of the evening. I'm going to have to cancel. If you hear from Strazzo, could you get him to call me?"

"Uh, I've already heard from him. I was going to mention it when we had supper this evening."

"Can we discuss it over the phone?" Vincenzo asked, distracted by the public relations nightmare going on in front of him on the television.

Sondra huffed loudly into the phone, her voice sharp and piercing. "Why not. It seems you

Eton boys have no qualms about discussing delicate things over the phone rather than in person. Your brother called. Sounded like someone sucked the wind right out of him. Then he proposed, Vincenzo. Who the hell does that? Over the phone, no less!"

"What?" Vincenzo sat back in his chair stunned. His brother's idea of commitment was wearing his boxer briefs two days in a row.

"That's what I said. Of course, I gave him an earful. Then, I see this. He's a loose cannon, Vincenzo. Did you watch the broadcast all the way through?"

Vincenzo went silent, thinking of how Sondra had called his brother a hothead. "No, I didn't watch it entirely," he remarked, looking at the remnants of his cell's shattered screen.

"Well, you should. The Evening Six is putting their slant on it at the expense of a battered woman. They're posturing, calling for Strazzo's arrest, trying to sway popular opinion with the byline that another rich kid is getting off with a misdemeanor for what they erroneously think accounts for aggravated assault."

"At least that'll soften the blow when I tell him I've been instructed to cut him free from the company." Vincenzo twirled a pen in his fingers, snapping the top in and out.

"Ha. That's going to go over like a lead zeppelin."

"Yeah, we nearly came to blows about where we were going to take the company tech-wise two months ago. I've always been able to smooth things over with the board—he's going to see this as my routing him from the company. What's more, he would've been happy to hear the direction the meeting took today. Had he been there. We're moving forward with the idea he pitched after Dad died."

"Who knew, maybe hot stuff has a head for business after all."

"Not that he's ever showed any interest in it. I swear he only comes to meetings to argue with me. Anyhow, I'd better go," Vincenzo said, relieved to have the excuse to cancel.

He still needed to get ahead of the news if he could and have the sit-down Emilia offered earlier. The weight that hung across his shoulders lifted, thinking of how good she'd felt in his arms and the fresh fragrance of her light perfume.

He'd go to Galveston. Beg her to see him if he had to. At worst, he'd spend the night away from the press that hounded him. At best, he'd throw a couple of dollars in a slot machine and have a couple of bourbons to ease the tension of the day away.

Either way, it was a win-win proposition.

The return trip to Galveston was shorter than it seemed as Vincenzo reviewed his and Emilia's interactions. He didn't want to think the worst of her, but he scarcely believed fate had thrown him together with the woman who had stripped his father of his dignity, and now was poised to hammer the last nail into Hex Holding's coffin.

He removed her pearls and scarf from his pocket and thought of the sincerity in her voice when she'd confessed she hadn't known about the business connection. In the moment, he'd felt so betrayed. But now, having had time to clear his head, he realized that she may have been as surprised as he was.

As the imperfect seeds slid through his fingers, he thought of them lying flat against her skin. How his lips had lingered along her collar bone as he suckled their uneven surface. He thought of how she had folded the scarf and put it in his breast pocket. Her tipsy chatter and wild hair endearing her to him. Both items were a lot like her. The freshwater pearls were full of character. The scarf, like the hollow of her neck, sensually silken.

If he had any forethought at all, he would have given them to Danny at the meeting. He hadn't been certain if he wanted Emilia to call him as he'd laid his number on her pillow when he'd left her this morning. Now he was afraid to think what might happen if she never did again. After embarrassing her in the boardroom, he owed her an apology, and he shouldn't have waited so long to do so.

Palms damp, he dialed her number.

"Emilia speaking."

"It's Vincenzo. I'd like to take you up on your offer for lunch. I owe you an apology. And I'd like to do so in person." Sondra's words were banging around in his head about how the Eton brothers were quite comfortable doing things over the phone, which should be done in person.

Emilia's heart skidded to a halt at the sound of his voice. Her mouth full of cotton as she stumbled out her reply. "Yes, of course. I'll see you soon." Fluffing and finger-combing her hair, she gave one last glance in the mirror before strapping on a pair of heels.

Full of nervous energy, she paced and thought about her next actions. Undeniably attracted to the man, she needed to put a stop to the ridiculousness of the situation. She didn't have time to catch feelings. She needed to forget him. He was as good as engaged, and despite the fact she hadn't stopped thinking of him since they'd met, she would excise him from her life.

Danny would handle the Houston branch from now on. She'd wash her hands of all the meetings. There would be no chance of crossover between the two of them ever again. They'd apologize, and resume a professional relationship. "There, settled. No problem," Emilia said aloud in her empty hotel room. After tonight, Vincenzo Eton would cease to exist in her mind.

Glancing at the clock, she noticed that the hour for him to drive there had passed quickly. Keycard in hand, she exited her hotel room and brusquely made for the elevators.

***

Vincenzo watched Emilia glide across the lobby. His gaze locked on the rise and fall of her hips and the echo of her stilettos on the tiled flooring, then muffled as she crossed the patterned carpet floor of the casino like a runway model. She certainly looked the part—the hem of a lustrous royal blue satin dress showcasing her bronzed legs as it easily molded itself to the rest of her body. His mind's eye could see the hint of her breast and golden hips against the white of the hotel sheets from earlier that morning. Curtailing his thoughts from their lurid tailspin, he rose to greet her.

"Before I forget…" Vincenzo retrieved the folded scarf and pearls from an inner pocket and passed them into her hand.

As his fingers grazed her own, her resolve to wash her hands clean of him waivered, sunk by the memory of his gentle ministrations against the column of her throat. She tied the cheery fabric of her scarf artfully around her neck, secreting the strand of gems in her slim wallet. Awkwardly shifting from one foot to the other, Emilia offered an olive branch. "Very kind of you to come all this way to return these. They have enormous sentimental value, and I can't imagine how I've managed to lose one of them at least twice on this trip."

"Possibly stress," he mused. "Thank you for being gracious enough to meet with me."

"Think nothing of it." Noticing an unreadable expression on her face, Vincenzo assumed the worst. "So, you've seen the news, I presume?"

"Seen what, exactly?" she queried. She was yet blissfully unaware Strazzo was trending on viral media even more so than usual in the mere hours she had last met with Vincenzo.

"This is something best said over a drink. Would you like to get a coffee, or do you need something more substantial?" His voice was husky. His thoughts torn between business and an overwhelming lewd urge.

Seeing the familiar gleam of innuendo in his eyes, she felt a corresponding surge of desire in response. Her eyes darkened, her lips parting innocently as she bit the plump flesh of her lower lip. "You promised me the sights and sounds the night has to offer. Or, don't you remember?"

"I remember everything, Emilia. Come, I want to take you to Pleasure Pier."

"I bet you do," Emilia muttered under her breath, the timbre of his voice sending a delicious shiver up her spine.

Vincenzo's gaze captured hers, the look on his countenance that of a satisfied cat who had licked the meat clean off the canary.

They arrived at Pleasure Pier and walked down the promenade until they reached a bistro-style restaurant. While the restaurant bustled with customers, Vincenzo easily commandeered a table. They followed behind the waitress as she directed them to a generously sized table for two. They took their place in the cheery red chairs under a trellis laden with bright flowers.

"I'll have the Caesar, topped with Cajun chicken. And sparkling water if you have it." At the waitress' smile and nod, Emilia added, "Thank you." Emilia smiled at the waitress with a twinge of compassion for the young woman. She looked run ragged. Her section of the restaurant was exceedingly busy. Emmi had worked similar jobs to put herself through college, working upwards of seventeen hours a day sometimes.

Vincenzo asked for nachos heaped with peppers, black olives, and jalapenos, all dressed in a sharp gooey cheese. Relatively simple fare, considering the net worth of the two individuals at the table. The waitress smiled and ducked off to relay their order to the cook.

Vincenzo wondered how best to tell Emilia of Strazzo's fight before she discovered it for herself, but first, his conscience demanded he make things right with Emilia. "As I mentioned, I want to apologize. I behaved unprofessionally. There's no excuse for it."

"No, there isn't. However, we both behaved poorly, which lessens our credibility in the eyes of those we're leading." Taking the cloth napkin from the table, Emilia spread it out onto her lap and rearranged her cutlery.

"I agree." Vincenzo watched as the waitress returned with their drinks and bustled off again. "As to the subject matter itself, I've given that considerable thought as well—"

Before he could continue, Emilia cut him off in an attempt to cover her embarrassment and save face. "What we did…was a mistake."

Vincenzo's heart plunged, not expecting her to say those words. He waited for her to speak further, undecided what he should say in response.

"It was a moment of weakness, and I deeply regret it. I hope you can figure things out with Sondra and, don't worry, it's not my place to tell her anything. I'll leave that up to you." She took a sip of her seltzer water to busy her hands.

For a moment, Vincenzo was confused. Then, remembering how his mother had called Sondra his fiancée, he jumped in to clarify. "We're not together," he blurted.

Emilia nearly spit out her drink, the sparkling water bubbles going up her nose. "But I thought she was your…?"

"She's not. She never was." He searched her face for any sign of feelings toward him now that she knew the truth.

"And your supper plans…?"

"Those were real, but not in the way you might imagine. And I've canceled them to be here with you." Vincenzo took a deep breath, readying himself to explain everything. "Sondra has been a friend of the family—well, Strazzo's, really—for many years now. As I'm sure you have figured out, Strazzo isn't really the settling down type. So, the family has pushed us together instead. We've gone on a few dates, but…" he trailed off for a moment. "I'm not sure if there's anything there. She's a wonderful woman, I'm just not sure she's the one for me."

She sputtered and redirected, unsure what to feel about all of this just yet. "You said there was a new development regarding the merger. I'm curious what it is." She sipped her water more carefully, watching him over the rim of the glass.

Vincenzo was brought back to Strazzo's latest antic. "I'd rather not discuss it during dinner, I fear it will leave us both with indigestion," he remarked as the waitress approached the table with their food. "Instead, now that the air has been cleared, let's start with a few questions to get to know each other a bit better."

"That might not be for the best, I tend to interrogate people. Or at least, so I've been told." Emilia smiled, thinking of a date she had gone on before meeting her husband.

"You? Interrogate? I can't even begin to imagine."

"Well, how else am I supposed to get to know someone if I can't ask them questions?"

"Try me. What's one of the questions you'd ask a potential date?"

"Honestly, I'd go straight to for the throat. Religion, politics, and abortion."

Vincenzo let out a long, low whistle. "Do you get ghosted a lot?" He chuckled, then sipped his coffee.

Emilia surprised him, letting out a warm peal of laughter. "Danny says I'm too much, and I intimidate men. If he were here now, he'd probably be offering coaching advice."

"Well, what's your answer regarding these topics?" Vincenzo stalled, not wanting the easy mood between them to change, knowing the moment they began discussing Strazzo, Emilia Patric would change hats and become CEO.

"In truth, I think they're broad and nuanced. Which isn't to say I don't have strongly held opinions about them myself."

"That's a very dignified answer, which tells me nothing. You'd make a good politician."

"Doubtful. I tell the truth, even if it comes at a cost to myself. I think it says something that speaks to my innate character. That I can have strong opinions about a topic, and not feel the need to spew my rhetoric to all who will listen."

"Noble, but not very practical."

"On some topics, no. It takes a lot of energy to hold two conflicting ideas in your mind and examine them both without bias. Often, opposing sides speak to their bias and never look for the middle ground. There are more similarities than there are differences. We just need to find something both sides can agree on."

"And that right there is what makes you an excellent CEO."

Emilia smiled at his compliment, as the waitress came to clear the table of their plates. "Could you bring the check with you when you return, please?"

"Yes, of course. I'll be right back." The exhausted waitress let out another genuine smile, despite the fact that she was ready for her shift to end.

"Here's another question for you, will your ego let me pick up the tab?" Emilia grinned, putting him on the spot.

"It's high time you paid for something. I've already had you over to my mother's and you nearly ate us out of house and home," he bandied back with an easy, sexy smile. "I'll wait for you outside."

Emilia watched as the waitress interacted with the other hosts, easily directing them. She observed as the young woman mentally checked the tally for accuracy before bringing the check to her.

"Here's the bill," the waitress said, trying to not look as though her evening meal depended on the tips she earned that night.

"Trick question, think fast… If you had a fairy godmother, what would you ask her for? I understand you're tired, but I'm interested in hearing your answer to this."

Not wanting to engage yet another customer who thought their small talk was the wittiest thing since sliced cheese, the waitress answered as succinctly as possible. "I'd like enough money to start a ranch for troubled teens."

Taking the debit machine in hand, Emilia squared away her bill and left a generous tip. "Ah, a woman after my own heart. Here's my business card," she said, handing it over to the confused waitress. "Come see me on Monday. If you have any questions, an internet search engine should help you with most of what you'd like to know about my company. If you don't show, I'll know you're not serious about the ranch."

Leaving the girl gaping after her, Emilia left the restaurant. Spying Vincenzo sitting on a bench waiting for her, a twinge pinched her heart. She thought of how many times Mason had waited for her as she worked.

Seeing her, Vincenzo stood to join her. They crossed the road to the sandy expanse. Emilia stooped to pull off her heels and took the hand Vincenzo offered out to her. He thought of how beautiful she looked under the Texas sky as they set off along the beach.

Twenty minutes later, he could no longer resist as he pulled her to him beneath Pleasure Pier and kissed her until she saw stars. It was then Vincenzo spied the muted shine of the photographer's lens.

It's a Small World, After All

Up until the reporter spotted the eldest of the two Eton's, the sultry evening yielded nothing of note for the semi-retired correspondent—save his fleshy hand draped around a cold glass of Guinness as he watched an old television slung atop the line of liquor bottles above the bartender. The entertainment section of the local news rambled on regarding the youngest Eton's altercation with predictable repetitiveness.

The best the reporter expected that afternoon was the prattle of a few oldies like himself who thought journalism was best accomplished in the streets and between the sheets. His evening would wind up as it typically did—jawing about the deplorable, downward spiral of left-wing, right-wing politically slanted news.

What he hadn't anticipated was a veritable scoop, which appeared when his eyes lit on staunch-lipped Vincenzo Eton stepping out with a mystery woman. The man's thin, greasy mustache practically twitched with glee when he'd spotted the duo canoodling.

He'd stepped off his barstool, leaving a couple bills on the bar to pay off his debt, and followed them along the beach. He was rewarded with several scandalous photos as they got down and dirty in a shallow pool offshore.

"Care to make a statement, Mr. Eton?" the peeping pervert said from behind his camera as he continued to snap their photo, trying to get a shot of his lady friend who was busy pulling the scarf over her face and the front of her dress together.

"You nosy son of a—" Vincenzo stepped in front of the photographer's line of sight, took one of the shoes he had been carrying, and whipped them at the reporter, cheering internally as one of them bounced off the man's head.

"Attempted assault!" the reporter shrieked, switching his tune to intentional destruction of property when Vincenzo tore the camera from his grasp.

"Guess you shouldn't have been pointing it at my private business then," Vincenzo snarled.

"It ain't private if you're doing it on the beach, son," the man quipped, thinking the Eton brothers had done him a favor today. Grabbing what was left of his camera, he hightailed it out of there.

***

Observing Vincenzo's look of chagrin, Emilia patted his hand. "Well, Cinderella, I think you got the better of that fight. Are you certain it didn't wash away?" Emmi asked while they combed the beach in tandem looking for the mate to the single dark leather shoe in Vincenzo's hand.

"Some ugly stepsister's nabbed it by now," he said, playing along with the reference. "After all, the woman who finds the shoe and places it on my foot gets…" he paused, lecherously eyeing her up, thinking about what he'd like to give her.

"Gets what?" Emmi asked, wondering what he'd do to her if she found his shoe.

"This," he used the opportunity to draw her to him, his hand gently cupping the side of her face as he kissed her forehead before venturing lower to capture her lips in a sweet kiss.

"Not worth my time. It'll need to stay lost." She pulled away, trying to stomp out the spark of something that scared the hell out of her.

Love, her heart whispered. Not possible. What she'd had with Mason was a statistical improbability. A miracle. To find it twice in a lifetime? And in a day, no less. Not a chance.

Vincenzo made a low sound with an exaggerated clutch at his chest.

"What size do you wear?" she asked, an idea formulating in her mind.

"Eleven, why?"

"Give me your shoe. I'll be right back." She dashed across the street and entered the footwear depot.

The tinkle of the door swinging open alerted the diminutive associate standing in an aisle as she restocked the selection of women's footwear. Her gaze came to rest on a woman wearing an expensive blue dress, her attire more suited to a nightclub than that of a chain store that sold footwear. Yet, here she was.

Making her way over to the same aisle, the associate watched as the taller brunette attempted to pull down a pair of shoes from the top shelf. Coming from behind, she appeared at the woman's side with a step ladder. "Perhaps I can offer you some assistance?"

Emilia looked toward another attendant who stood chatting up his cashier coworker.

"Oh. Yes, please. I'm looking for a similar shoe," she said, holding the single shoe for the associate's perusal. "Size eleven. Thank you."

The woman looked at the shoe, recognizing it immediately. *It couldn't be.* Her voice rose in a near shout as she questioned this stranger, "Please explain to me why you have my husband's shoe?" Even after she'd left Vincenzo, she still had feelings for him.

It was Emilia's turn to look disconcerted. A corresponding blush formed across her cheeks, as her gaze darted to see if any were around to witness her shame. "Your husband's shoe?"

"Yes. My husband, Vincenzo Eton," the woman said, folding her arms across her chest. "You won't find this shoe here in America. This is an Italian shoe, handmade leather upper." She turned the shoe over in her tiny hand. "See here? This marking on the sole? It identifies a particular brand of rubber only sold in Europe. I should know. I'm the one who purchased them for him."

"I…I…don't doubt you did. Vincenzo—my friend—was in a dust-up, and the ocean seems to have taken the other shoe out to sea. I… wasn't aware he had a wife."

Vincenzo crossed the road barefoot and peered into the store's window, spotting Emilia talking with a woman several inches shorter than herself. As the woman turned, the color drained from his face. Uncaring whether he was turfed from the strip mall, he burst into the store and ran to Emilia's side.

"Isabella." Vincenzo's voice broke with emotion thinking of the last time he'd seen her face, one year and three months ago.

For what felt like the third time on this particular vacation, Emilia felt like the hand of fate had ripped her from one spot to another, manipulating the weave of her life as the ground seemed to fall away under her. Glaring at him, eyes ablaze with anger, she delivered a resounding slap across his face, hard enough to leave a red welt on his cheek.

Dropping the box of shoes she held in hand, Emilia fled the store.

"Emilia, please," Vincenzo begged over the third voicemail he'd left her over the last few days. "Call me back. We have much to discuss. There's an explanation for everything, I promise." He ran his hands through his hair and leaned back in his chair.

The intercom buzzed as his receptionist informed him of Strazzo's arrival. "Send him in," he said, a new wave of stress settling on his shoulders as he carefully planned out the words to let his brother go from the company as delicately as he could.

The coming weeks yielded long hours of preparatory work for the ribbon-cutting ceremony of her foundation, which Emilia gratefully threw herself into in an attempt to forget everything.

Deleting the latest voicemail he'd left her without playing it, Emilia had chosen not to answer any of his calls. She couldn't trust herself to speak with him and be able to resist the lies she so desperately wanted to believe. Her only concern with him anymore would be on a professional level, and anything of that nature could go through Danny.

Vincenzo had lied to her. He also had a wife. Perhaps he was lying about Sondra also. A wife and a fiancée—two different women. *What have I gotten myself in the middle of?* Emilia didn't know what to believe anymore, but her already delicate heart couldn't handle this. Vincenzo had been the first person she'd been with, and the first person she developed real feelings for, since Mason. But now she knew she was just another notch in the rich man's belt.

She was relieved when the time came, one month later, to check out of her hotel and fly home. She was firmly intent on putting Vincenzo behind her, seeing no reason to contact him.

Until the morning sickness began.

Four months later…

Strazzo strolled into class and chose a seat near the back of the classroom, having completed most of his courses online out of the way of prying eyes. He appeared in class for the first time in five years, namely because of the name on the presentation billing. It was remarkable how unchanged the school was since he last attended, right down to the same well-worn suit jacket the professor wore.

Sun shone into the room, catching the falling dust motes. Looking around, he felt the weight of his age. Though he was at best five years older than most of the student body, his father's death and the subsequent responsibility that came with it had aged him, lending him distinctive maturity when he finally addressed the grief which plagued his heart.

He'd been stone-cold sober for seven months and counting, ever since the ring shop incident. He'd had a surprising conversation with his brother four months back, in which they both agreed that he should leave Hex Holdings and pursue his dreams of becoming a doctor. Strazzo never would have guessed how well his brother would take the news, and it completely bowled him over when Vincenzo showed such exuberant support. Feeling like a new man, the only thing that weighed on Strazzo was his brother's most recent announcement.

"I think it's high time to settle down," Vincenzo had said to Strazzo and Vitoria at a family dinner a couple months ago. "And Sondra is a fine woman with which to do so." At first, he'd thought Vincenzo was suggesting Strazzo and Sondra were meant to be, and he was eager to share his recent realization of the same conclusion.

But just as Strazzo was about to open his mouth, Vincenzo had motioned for Sondra to enter from the doorway, putting his arm around her shoulders as she flashed the blinding rock at Strazzo and Vitoria. With a smile, Vincenzo had said, "The wedding will be in the spring."

Shaking his head slightly, Strazzo brought himself out of the nightmare of a memory.

His classes were in the bowels of the sciences building, in one of the original buildings that made up the expansive campus. Its brickwork and vines held a legacy of over one hundred years in its hallways of turning out brilliant students who went on to serve in occupations the world over. As he sat waiting for his course to begin, he found himself staring at the almost unnoticeable baby bump of his old brother's old flame, Emilia Patric.

After a brief introduction, Emilia took over the class. "Thank you for having me, Professor," she said as she put up her first slide. "Good afternoon class, my name is Emilia. It will be my distinct pleasure to present to you the latest detection methodologies offered by our product lines. You might even be wondering what semiconductors and applications in biology have in common. Rest assured, your questions will be answered."

Strazzo watched her presentation with interest as she discussed the body of her work and concluded in the ninety minutes she'd been given. Making his way to the front of the class, he waited patiently for the other students to ask their questions and depart.

"Emilia," he said simply.

Emilia's heart skipped at the familiar voice, relieved to see Strazzo instead of Vincenzo.

"Hello, Strazzo. A wonderful surprise to see you here this morning. I don't think I knew you were attending medical school?" Emilia was thankful she wasn't showing significantly yet, hoping he wouldn't notice.

"I…just returned," he answered hesitantly before attempting to change the topic. "I thought you left Houston?" The sound of a girl's pen scratching across her pad of paper, still writing the notes that filled up the overhead projection screen, kept him from speaking more candidly.

"I did. I just flew in—the professor called in a special favor for this subject matter, as I'm an expert in the field. I knew the professor when we were undergraduates together, and had agreed to do this way back then. I guess it was time to fulfill that promise."

"She's only telling you part of the story," the robust professor interjected, returning from the supply closet on the far side of the room. "She lost a bet regarding my mustache."

"Ugh, you mean the poor excuse for dental drapes hovering over your perfectly good lips? Or the off-center goatee?" Emilia rolled her eyes with a friendly smile.

Strazzo laughed, a hearty boom echoing through the lecture hall.

"I know when I'm beaten. I'll leave you two to catch up." The professor grabbed his briefcase and headed toward the door.

"Care to get that coffee you offered me five-ish months ago?" Strazzo asked. His mature mannerism at odds with what Emilia had seen of him previously. This Strazzo was almost sedate by comparison.

No notes of seduction or ulterior motive in his tone, Emmi agreed. "I'd love to. Let me get my coat." Emilia walked to the coat stand offset from the door and plucked her coat from its spindles.

They settled in a small coffee shop not far from campus. Sitting across from him, she couldn't believe the complete one-eighty he had done. Maturity had settled over his shoulders like a familiar coat. Gone was the cocksure young man, and she wasn't sure where he had locked his bad-assery away. Nor was she sure she liked it entirely, as she listened to what he had to say with a heavy heart.

"Shortly before we met you, Vincenzo had just heard from the police. His wife had been missing for a little over a year. They were closing her case file, all the leads gone cold. And after such a long time, she was presumed to either be dead or not wanting to be found. They suggested he file for a divorce so he could move on with his life. Vincenzo had just come to terms with everything when there you were."

Emilia's eyes were scrunched in scrutiny. "Okay, you've completely lost me. I met Vincenzo's wife—Isabella."

"Yes, but what you didn't know at the time was she had been gone for over a year. After our pops died, Vincenzo started realigning his life with his immediate family, not wanting to regret anything further. But this didn't sit well with Isabella, since she and Mama were always at each other's throats. Don't get me wrong, not everything was Isabella's fault. In Mama's eyes, there wasn't a lot Isabella could do right. Mama felt like she had taken her baby boy away from her, and the relationship had been doomed from the start. Eventually, Isabella caved under the pressure, and left."

"You mean like…she just left? Without a word?" Emilia shifted uncomfortably in her chair. Vitoria was a strong-headed matriarch. She had suspected Vitoria was nice, so long as you saw eye to eye with her.

"Yep. Dropped off the face of the map, presumed dead. Gone."

"Or working at a shoe shop in Galveston." Emilia's lips pursed with incredulity. "Forgive me if this story seems a little far-fetched. People don't just go around disappearing."

"I know, it seems odd. Imagine Vincenzo's reservations when, in one fell swoop, you got in a shuttle that led straight to his place, found his missing wife, and then coincidentally turned out to be the CEO locking horns with his company."

Emilia looked up at the ceiling and nodded her head. "Well, it's one heck of a perfect storm, I'll give you that. But the only thing I did with intent was get on the chartered plane to Houston for something completely unrelated to any of that. The rest is merely coincidence, weird or otherwise."

Strazzo reached out across the table and patted Emmi's hand. "I believe you, even if Vincenzo doesn't."

"Well, thank you. Come to think of it, my late husband and I missed each other by weeks or years, always living in the same area, frequenting the same places, until one fateful day when we finally met."

"Why didn't you answer any of Vincenzo's calls? I tried talking to him about you, but he's been incredibly tight-lipped. What happened between you two?"

"I don't think it matters now, do you? He's already got two women jostling for his affections, right?"

Strazzo shook his head. "Isabella left again, this time telling him she didn't intend to see him ever again. She moved to Montana."

"Oh." Emilia's heart scuttled out from the corner it had hidden in. Peeking its proverbial head out, hopeful there might be a resolution to the pain it felt.

"There's something else you should know."

Emilia was pretty sure what was coming next, noticing that Strazzo had only mentioned Isabella so far. "What's that?"

"Vincenzo's getting married."

So, they were engaged, Emmi thought. Her cheeks flushed with anger at his blatant lies and nonchalant ability to involve her in his infidelity.

"If you're planning on telling him you're with child, you should probably do it soon."

I do?

Two months later…

Vincenzo stood in the backyard of his mother's house, ready to say "I do" to a woman he wasn't fully convinced he loved. More, he resigned himself to his fate, thinking it would be better to marry than to remain alone. His end of the bargain wasn't bad. Sondra was perfect, and ticked every box. If it weren't for the time he'd shared with Emilia, perhaps he could have learned to love her. His family, for the most part, were present and accounted for. All, except Strazzo.

***

Strazzo and Emilia pulled up in front of the family home. She'd called him the evening before after having some time to think about it and asked him to collect her from the airport.

"Are you sure you want to do this here and now, Emilia?" Strazzo asked. It was getting harder to hide the bump, but still, she'd said nothing.

Emmi noted something in his youthful vigor had changed since she'd seen him last.

Thinking if they still spoke after this, maybe she'd ask him why. "I have to. I think?" she said questioningly, wrestling with herself and thinking how selfish she was to come here and do this on this day.

"I don't think this is going to end the way you think it will. Vincenzo abhors drama. He's very much like our father. Not just old school—think first century. *Ancient* school," Strazzo said, a tinge of worry across his face. Even he couldn't predict how his older brother would react.

"If not now, when? I need to be clear about my feelings. I have to know." Emmi's heart hung heavy in her chest, knowing she should have called him sooner. Then, a look of resolve crossing her face, she added, "At the very least, he deserves to know." Her hand subconsciously caressed her belly.

Emmi thought of how many times she wanted to answer Vincenzo's calls, imagining he had either picked up where he'd left off with his wife or lied about being engaged to Sondra, praying whatever she felt would go away. Strazzo continued to throw out all the questions she'd already asked herself.

"And you couldn't have thought to ask your question before the wedding date?" Strazzo paced back and forth. Trying to determine if he should warn Vincenzo, or let it play out. Maybe Emmi wouldn't go through with it. Oh, but he hoped she would. Thinking of Sondra getting dressed in her wedding gown, Strazzo kicked himself for being blind for so long to something that had been right in front of him.

When he'd tried again to tell her that he loved her, she pushed him away…again. In a last ditch effort, the big question burst from his lips on the phone, and Sondra had given him an earful before hanging up. But it would crush his heart to just let her walk down the aisle and marry his brother. He had to get her to realize he was sincere.

He also had to admit, Emmi had more guts than he. He had been pining for Sondra for the better part of seven months now, holding onto that diamond ring she'd jokingly asked him to buy for her, yet unable to work up the courage to say more than he had on the phone.

Emmi threw her gaze up at the sky, lifting her arms in a defeated gesture. "I didn't know what to say. But I realize now, I've already lost one man I loved. I don't want to lose another. At least, not without a fight."

Strazzo shrugged his shoulders, feeling exactly what she did. "Then, I guess it's now or never."

Entering the wedding wonderland in fashionably late style, Strazzo and Emilia took their seats. Emilia's eyes sought out Vincenzo at the front of the aisle. He stood near the wedding arch, which hung with cattleya orchids, purple and white lilies, and lilac-colored china asters. His suit was a coal-black blend with wide double-breasted lapels. He had a black-and-white striped tie folded into the vest's light gray satin. A tie pin fixed the look together, as did the cuff links he wore. He looked so handsome, but did Emilia detect a hint of unease from him?

Vincenzo shifted his weight from foot to foot, subtly wringing his hands together in a nervous gesture. The bride waited in the wings, her face hidden by the veil as Vincenzo's eyes scoured the crowd in search of Strazzo. As their gaze met, Vincenzo's eyes narrowed when they passed over the woman who had turned his life upside down. *How dare she show up here.*

Though, she did look like she was glowing. He noticed her dark hair falling past her shoulders like fine silk. Vincenzo's disdain faltered when he saw her smile at him. Did he see sadness behind it? Her smoky eyes pierced into his soul, and instantly, memories of their short time together came flooding back.

His best man coughed discreetly to catch his attention when the Wedding March began playing. Vincenzo tore his gaze away from Emmi and redirected it to his intended, but his thoughts remained on Emmi. *She refused my calls all those months ago. Why did Emilia wait so long to allow me back in her life? What could she possibly be here for?* His curiosity shortly turned to hurt and anger.

Vincenzo's mind raced with questions while he tried to plaster on a smile in Sondra's direction, playing the part of the happy groom. His vision blurred, his focus elsewhere. Sondra drew close, ready to exchange their vows and make this permanent. Her visage appeared to Vincenzo as Emilia, and for a brief moment, he wondered what could have been. Eyes hardening, he cleared his vision. *Well,* he thought with resolve. *She can just keep it to herself. It's too late.*

In her seat, Emmi vibrated with anxiety. Heart hammering in her throat as the faint refrain of the wedding music began, its haunting notes filling the yard with as much sorrow as her heart contained.

Sondra looked a vision as she began her glide down the aisle, her dark curls swept up in seed pearls, her dress exquisite with its extensive train. In that moment, Emilia had a crisis of conscience. *What if Sondra loves Vincenzo as much as I do? I can't break up a marriage!*

Turning abruptly to Strazzo, her heart beating in her throat, she whispered, "I shouldn't be here, Strazzo. What right do I have to come and ruin their day? I can't do this to them." She made herself as small as possible, sinking into her chair behind the person who sat in front of her. Looking around like a trapped rat, Emmi planned to sneak out the side of the tent at the first opportunity she got. "Give me the fob to your car. I'll wait there till my cab arrives."

Not knowing what to say, whether he should stop her or allow her to leave, Strazzo deflated and handed Emmi the black nub to his sports car. He watched as she slid out of the palatial tent's side opening, realizing too late that he had been depending on her to help both of them. Looking forward, he watched as his brother held onto the hands of the woman *he* was meant to marry.

Emilia slid into the passenger seat of Strazzo's car and wept bitterly, letting the tears she'd been fighting for months flow freely. So involved in her emotions, Emmi didn't see the man standing outside the car door. A brisk knock on her window jolted her out of her one-woman pity party. The man's face was recognizable in an instant.

"What are you doing here?"

Strazzo looked at the tawny skin of Sondra Perric's back as she stood next to Vincenzo. She was moment's away from being his brother's bride. He groaned. *My brother's bride, not mine.*

Her voluptuous shape and round buttocks outlined in crepe silk were almost too much for him to bear. White and rose gold drop earrings with discreet diamonds swung on their delicate chains. Her dark curly hair was carefully arranged into a spray of off-white freshwater pearls, her skin a delicious line of contrast between shoulders and gown.

A sinking feeling crept into his heart. Sondra had been his friend for three years. When he was drunk, high, temporarily incarcerated, she'd always shown up. She even flew to Reno once to collect him after he'd lost his wallet in a narcotics-fueled rage. By the time he'd clawed his way back to sobriety and all of that was behind him, she had moved on.

"Dearly beloved, today we are gathered to witness the union of Vincenzo Eton and Sondra

Perric." The justice of the peace spoke to those who shifted in their seats with barely contained excitement.

Strazzo shifted in his seat with building anxiety. The words of the ceremony echoed in his mind while beads of sweat formed on his forehead.

"Above you are the celestial lights, below you the sanctity of earth. A reminder love should brightly burn while remaining steadfast."

Strazzo felt his heart beating faster and faster, pumping blood through his veins with increased urgency until he couldn't stand it any longer.

Shooting up from his seat, Strazzo shouted, his voice ringing firm and true. "Don't marry him!" He managed to sidestep the attendants who came at him in a flurry of coattails. He could hear the wind rustling the leaves of a nearby tree, all other voices halted in utter silence and shock. Dozens of eyes rested on him, watching, waiting to see what he would do next.

In what felt like a single flying step, Strazzo reached the bride and dropped to one knee, ready to confess his repressed feelings in front of Sondra and all those present. His eyes flicked ever so briefly toward Vincenzo. He knew his brother despised drama. He knew this would likely create a permanent wedge between them, but right now, he didn't care. All that mattered was that Sondra knew how he felt—how he truly felt—before it was too late.

"I've been a selfish idiot," he began. Sondra had dropped Vincenzo's hands and turned to face Strazzo. Her eyes searched his, her mouth slightly agape. *Are those tears in her eyes?* Remembering what he'd told Emmi before entering the tent, he tried to encourage himself. *It's now or never.* "Sondra, you gave freely of your warmth and affection. Always trustworthy, always there for me when I needed you most. My sweet, stout-of-heart Sondra. If you have any love for me, let me make my home with you, love you, make a family with you," he implored, pulling the ring from his inner coat. "You helped me to pick this out."

Finally finding her words, Sondra's eyes hardened upon the sight of the familiar box. She took a step back as she spoke. "Oh, this is rich

Or don't you think I'd recognize the ring you picked out for your mother?"

He pulled the lid of the box open. "I bought this a week after we were there. I've been trying to work up the courage to tell you I was serious. I did try to tell you, but you dismissed me. I didn't know how to prove that I meant it."

Sondra's heart thudded. She remembered laughing at him, certain he'd been teasing her, guarding her hopeful heart. *Is this really happening?* she wondered. *After all this time that I have loved him and dreamt of this moment, he is finally saying the words I've longed to hear. But, now? At my wedding?* Her mouth was incapable of forming words—he'd rendered her speechless. *I can't believe he went back and bought it.* She started to reach out to the ring, not sure what to say or do. She remembered how she'd jokingly proposed to him, tittering as she'd tried it on as though she were the blushing bride and he the handsome groom.

Her thoughts were interrupted by her brother. "Control your dog, Eton." He started toward Strazzo with murderous intent in his eyes.

Strazzo pushed away as two men tried to move him from his position in front of her.

"You're making a mistake." Eyes turning downcast for a moment, he admitted, "I made a mistake—I should have told you sooner. My life is changing, Sondra. I want you to be there to share it with me." Chaos broke out on the bride's side as one indignant person after another stood up in protest of Strazzo's actions.

"What kind of a sham show is this?" bellowed the bride's father. A look of sincere worry on his face. His baby girl was not marrying this irresponsible twat if he had anything to say about it.

Sondra's other brother stood at the ready, prepared to throttle Strazzo.

"I didn't mean to do this so…so publicly. Vincenzo left me no choice." He turned to his brother, a look of apology and desperation on his face. "I never thought you'd go through with it, bro. You were with Emmi. Sondra has been my best friend for years, but then I realized it was more than just friendship. By then, it was too late. You and Sondra were planning your wedding."

Vincenzo's hands clenched tightly, listening to his brother's words. He felt his cheeks flame red, unsure if he was truly upset with the halt to the ceremony, or simply embarrassed to have his business be so public.

Strazzo continued, "Emmi changed my mind. Not intentionally, of course. She loves you, Vincenzo. Her courage to come here to tell you, even though she couldn't go through with it, gave me the incentive I needed to make sure you don't marry the love of *my* life."

"At least she had the good sense to not disrupt the ceremony," Vincenzo ground out, hiding the butterflies that suddenly made an appearance in his stomach. "Which is more than I can say for my brother."

"I'm sorry, Vincenzo. Truly. But I couldn't hold this in any longer. No more secrets. And speaking of…" he trailed off for a moment, a meaningful look in his eyes. "You should go find Emmi. There's unfinished business, Vincenzo."

"Emilia and I are done. She's made that very clear." Vincenzo felt the familiar heartache creep in as he searched the sea of faces for her, thinking of her sad smile before he had looked away earlier.

The officiant tried to calm people down as they milled about high in emotion and short on temper.

His focus back on the bride, Strazzo continued to make his case. "Sondra, I want to dance with you on our fiftieth wedding anniversary and reminisce about how I begged you not to marry him. I want to talk about what an idiot I was for being blind to what was right in front of me. I want to hold your hands as we tell our great-grandkids the story of how we finally began our journey together."

Sondra stared into his pleading eyes, the tiny ring box still in his hand, his face contrite, his posture tense. *He's being sincere,* she realized.

Strazzo held the box with the glittering ring out to her. "Read the inscription," he begged her.

"Get the hell out of here, Strazzo!" Vincenzo slapped the ring from his brother's hand before Sondra could decide whether or not to take it. "Take that cheap trinket with you."

Misinterpreting his brother's words, Strazzo snapped. "You disgust me. She's waiting to have the discussion she should have had with you months ago." Strazzo motioned to the large tent opening. "She's waiting in my car for her cab. Do the right thing, man."

"She shouldn't have come." Vincenzo turned away, his head hanging from the weight of the conversation. Covering up his pain, he hardened his voice and steeled his eyes, cold as the words issued forth from his mouth. "It's too late. She had the opportunity. She chose not to take it."

After questioning her about her growing bump, Emmi had sworn Strazzo to secrecy, not wishing to push Vincenzo into anything until she was confident of his feelings for her. *Her request for discretion be damned,* he thought. Strazzo couldn't keep dancing around the truth any longer.

"Emmi's pregnant, bro," Strazzo burst out at last. "You, of all people, should know what it is to bear a blow like the one you've slapped Emmi with." He hoped the news would spur Vincenzo into acting in her best interest, and ultimately his.

A vein popped on Vincenzo's forehead as a wave of chatter coursed through the crowd. Everyone hung on the brothers' interchange of words. Strazzo never disappointed to turn any family event into a dramafest of the finest caliber. Vincenzo tried to process his brother's words. *I'm going to be a father?*

"Whose bun is in whose oven?" whispered Vincenzo's eighty-year-old great aunt.

Vitoria leaned in and spoke into her ear. "Vincenzo's been baking in someone else's oven. You haven't met Emilia yet, my love. You'll adore her."

"Oh, dear," her aunt said with comic simplicity. Vitoria stifled a giggle and patted her aunt's knee.

Seeing the look of shame in Sondra's eyes at this new twist of news, Strazzo couldn't bear to hurt her any longer. He tore out of the tent, leaving the ring discarded somewhere on the ground. He beelined for the ostentatious ride he owned, its orange finish gleaming among the black and silver everyone else drove. Peering through the window as he approached, he felt suddenly alone in his pain.

Emilia had gonc.

Her wedding in shambles, Sondra called for a short time out, noticing that Vincenzo too could use a break from everything. He kindly offered his office for her to think things through privately, given the weight of his brother's confession. Vincenzo planned to take a walk. As they exited the tent, they left their guests wondering if there was going to be a wedding at all.

Sondra's bridesmaid entered the office behind her. Sondra didn't bother looking up, her back to her friend as she offered support. "I can't believe that cow showed up to crash your wedding."

"But, she didn't," Sondra said softly. She didn't hold anything against Emilia. She was mortified, sure. But maybe this was for the best. Maybe she wasn't meant to be with Vincenzo after all. Her eyes raised to meet those of her friend. "You saw what happened. That was all Strazzo. A year ago, I would have given anything to hear him say the words he did just now. But today… His timing is in poor taste, and I see it as another grab for attention."

The bridesmaid searched Sondra's face. "Do you have any feelings for him at all?"

"I'm not sure." Inside, everything was screaming at her that she did. But *should* she? Sondra found herself silently wondering if she had the necessary feelings required for Vincenzo even. She turned the ring box over in her hand, still uncertain why she had collected it from the ground after her intended slapped it out of Strazzo's hand.

"Maybe looking at the ring he chose will help. Didn't he say there was some sort of inscription?"

Sondra opened the box and stared at the ring she had modeled for him nearly a year prior. Its brilliance was almost blinding as it caught the sun that leaked into the room. Plucking the circle from its velveteen cocoon, she flipped it upside down to read the secret message.

Saint Sondra, Patron Saint of Strazzo, forever.

The words took her back to the jewelry store when she'd first known she loved the incorrigible troublemaker. Trying on the ring, the joke to get married had spilled out without any premeditated meaning behind it. But once the words had slipped past her lips, she realized that they stemmed from a place of truth. *I love him.* She thought of his phone call when he asked to take her on a date. She also thought of the phone call when he'd proposed. As inelegant as both moments were, he had tried to tell her how he felt and she had missed it. Or rather, she'd shut him down, building a wall around her heart. *I love him,* she thought again. *And he loves me.*

Sondra stood with purpose and walked out of Vincenzo's office without another word, knowing what she needed to do.

The rental car came to a halt in front of a picturesque cabin situated off Lake Livingston not far from Pointblank, Texas. Idyllic waves lapped the shore nearby as a two-person bench swing swayed in the evening breeze, its wooden frame lit only by a slit of moonlight on the water.

Emmi entered wordlessly through the door, her companion following behind her. She passed by the sunny, yellow tweed couch and ottoman in the living room on her way to the kitchen. A whimsical navy-blue pillow with a hand-drawn fish that advised her to "Go Jump in the Lake" rounded out the nautical motif as the clock in the shape of a ship's helm struck ten.

Grabbing herself a glass of orange juice, she laid down on the couch and closed her weary eyes.

Choking awake sometime later, Emmi stared blindly into the darkness of the room. Placing her feet on the floor, she noticed the distinct smell of cigar and the glow of its ember.

"Going somewhere?" Danny asked nonchalantly, taking a long drag from the slim cigar.

Emilia let out a squeak of surprise. Startled to hear his voice ring out in the darkness. "What are you still doing here?"

"Something you should have done." He ignored the rest of her questions, and crushed out his cigar in a nearby ashtray, its embers dying out. Stepping out onto the veranda, he motioned for Emilia to follow as he went around the side of the house toward the sound of a vehicle approaching.

"Danny," Emilia called to him with a heavy sigh. "I'm really not in the mood for games." She followed him outside anyway and was relieved, yet surprised, when she recognized the man who pulled up the long driveway.

"St. Haire?!" Emilia hadn't seen him since Mason's funeral. Others hopped out of the vehicle as a topless jeep wrangler rolled up. A woman exited the driver's seat with others in tow.

"Gunny, ya tall drink of water!" St. Haire called to her.

"Shut it, St. Haire. Before I string your saintly rabbit arse up," the woman crowed as she jumped out of the jeep and embraced him in a hug.

Emilia stared at the ragged company, excited to see her husband's old comrades, but confused as to why they were there. "Would someone please tell me what is going on?" Some she'd merely seen in a photo, others she vaguely recollected from her husband's funeral.

"Gladly, Patric. But only after he arrives," Danny said as he pointed down the driveway. His eye was trained on the last man to arrive.

A well-built man who looked like he could take his foe out with his pinky finger got out of the last vehicle, and approached the porch where Emilia and Danny stood. The soldiers all stood at attention, hands at a salute.

"Sir," Danny nodded.

Addressing Emmi, the commanding officer began speaking with a clipped cadence—a man of few precise words. "Mrs. Patric. Lieutenant Colonel Rodriguez. You've recently opened the North American Military Widows Foundation."

"Yes?" she questioned, trying to connect the dots.

"We're here to celebrate the grand opening," the commanding officer said, breaking into what Emmi figured was a rare smile.

"We wouldn't miss it for the world," St. Haire added.

Emilia sat back on the porch swing with a hard thud. "All of you came here just to be at the grand opening of the foundation?" She was overcome with emotion. It was almost like having Mason there with her. "And how are you involved in all this, Danny?"

Danny's eyebrows raised in mischief, but Gunny was the one to answer. "He was our insider," she said with a wink. "The CO asked me to reach out to you on the anniversary of

Mason's…" she trailed off. Emmi nodded at her, encouraging her to continue. "Anyway, I had to go through your frontlines," she said, motioning toward Danny before pointing a finger at Emilia. "You're a hard woman to track down!"

Everyone laughed as Danny added, "Imagine working for her!"

Emilia's eyes welled up as she looked at all of Mason's military buddies. "You remembered," she said, touched.

Lieutenant Colonel Rodriguez took back the reins. "Sergeant Patric was one of the best men I've ever commanded. I watched him sacrifice his safety countless times to save wounded men in the line of fire. I watched him lead other men into a burning building to save innocent civilians, watched him walk children to school to protect them. And I watched"—he paused, his lips quivering almost unnoticeably while he fought back his emotions—"as he lay down his life." Rodriguez looked pointedly into Emmi's eyes. "I would never forget a man like that."

"And any woman who is brave enough to tame that beast deserves our respects," Gunny added, trying to lighten the mood. A round of *oorahs* went around the soldiers.

My Sincerest Apologies

Eight days later…

"Vincenzo Eton, please."

Emmi glanced around at the lobby of Hex Holdings. Examining the sleek lines of the well-lit receptionist's desk, she admired the garden of small plants and various knick-knacks that embellished her space. She smiled inwardly at the poorly drawn pictures of what appeared to be animals on the woman's wall, knowing it wouldn't be long before hers were graced with the same.

"Do you have an appointment?" the woman asked as she pulled the viewscreen open on her computer to check his schedule.

"No, I was told he was in meetings," Emmi said. "I'd like to wait if I could."

"You can do anything you like, but I still need to let him know who wants to see him." The secretary's eyes skimmed to Emmi's belly, wondering if she was the one the rumors had been flowing about.

"Emilia Patric." She wondered if he'd even bother to come out to the lobby upon hearing her name.

Opting to stand, she paced the small area looking at the photos that graced the walls of the business throughout the ages. She saw pictures of the original building that housed Hex Holdings—much smaller than its current location. A picture of Vincenzo drew her closer. To the left of his picture was one of an older man with the same features, and to the left of his, an even grainier picture of another man in the Eton lineage.

Emilia understood why the company meant so much to Vincenzo—it was his family's legacy, something they had worked hard to get off the ground. She touched a hand to her belly. A legacy that rests on Vincenzo's shoulders to maintain and pass on.

Vincenzo ignored the internal office communicator's content as it blinked a notification, suspecting Strazzo had arrived early to discuss the final details before Emilia's arrival later.

"Gentlemen," he interrupted the thin weasel voice of a guy from accounting as he droned on about office incidentals. "We need to wrap up. I have a previous engagement."

As the meeting came to a close, Vincenzo popped back into his office to grab his coat. His desk was under several piles of paper, all of which needed addressing as soon as he got back from lunch. He thought about canceling, but he needed to make a few last-minute arrangements with Strazzo if the plans he had made were to go off without a hitch.

Emilia saw him first as he exited his office, his expression a stoic mask of unreadability. His hair had been trimmed in the latest style, and she cursed her emotions for getting the better of her. He looked as devastatingly handsome as ever as he strode down the hall, his gait even and purposeful. She saw the moment he realized she was standing there, but couldn't tell if he was happy to see her, or disgusted.

"Vincenzo," she said, trying to quell the thud-thumping of her heart and take control of the situation.

"Emilia." He looked at her for a long while, tension rising across his shoulders. He was startled to see her in place of his brother. "You're early. Very early."

Conscious of the work environs around them, Emilia licked her dry lips, and shifted from one foot to the next. A rise of color teased the apples of her cheeks. "Could we speak privately?"

"No." His answer came out more bluntly than he'd intended, his expression giving nothing away of the turmoil within as his gaze swept over her. His eyes were trained on her abdomen as if he might see his child moving within her. Seeing the hollowness in her eyes, his countenance softened. "What I mean is, I don't have time for this right now. I want to do this right. I didn't expect to see you until seven…at Mama's."

A nervous wreck for the next several hours, Emilia arrived at ten minutes to seven, wondering what Vincenzo would say to her. She was ushered directly into his home office and left alone. Half-heartedly, she scanned the room for a prominently placed picture of himself and his blushing bride on the corner of his desk. Or maybe atop the slat of the bookshelf, right alongside the tiny cacti. Not finding such a photo, her heart skipped a beat before she yanked herself back to reality. She had attended his wedding. It was delusional to imagine anything else.

She continued her survey. His décor was sparse. The walls held a smattering of tasteful paintings. There was a soft leather couch in a gray-blue color, and a solitary armchair in white. The selections impressed her. She'd taken him for a man who'd have selected a modern minimalist style. She wondered what else she might not know about him. A wall of books surrounded his desk. She hadn't pegged him for a regular reader.

Opting for the white chair, she took her seat as he entered and sat opposite her. "You must be curious why I'm here," she stated with resigned determination. Her thoughts crept toward the past, to the pleasant times they'd shared. For all the expectation she'd held in her heart, his presence wasn't as she'd imagined. Nor had she anticipated the uncomfortable tension that persisted between them.

"You crashed my wedding," he said curtly. "You haven't taken any of my calls." He paused, searching her face. "Yes. I do wonder what we could have to say to one another. You closed the door to anything between us." *And disappeared with my heart, just like Isabella.*

"If you're unwilling to listen, I shouldn't have come." Cursing herself for being old-fashioned and thinking that news that he was going to be a father should be the sort of thing worthy of being delivered in person.

His face remained expressionless, "You could've called when…" The tension in his voice was evident as he stepped away from her to pour a snifter of liquor. He turned, lifting his glass. "I'd offer you one, but you shouldn't drink in your condition."

"Then, you know?"

"Yes, although it would have been nice to hear it directly from you. Have you decided what you'll do?" he asked as he attempted to numb his nerves with the amber liquid that slid down his throat.

Emilia felt a stab of pain at his words. *It's a baby, not a broken coffee cup.* Feeling her emotions grow guarded, she answered in a professional manner. "I have. If you wish to be a part of the child's life, we can make an arrangement once the baby is born. You have my number. I'll answer this time." She stood and turned to leave.

"Wait," he said, realizing he was losing her again. Emilia paused as he motioned for her to join him on the couch. Gently, he reached over and touched her knee. "What about an arrangement now?"

She shied away from his touch, frigid and cold, none of the warmth she had displayed months ago. "Please keep your hands to yourself."

He removed his hand awkwardly. "I'd like to make a proposal."

She watched him with narrowed eyes, arms crossed across her body, unwilling to accept anything he might say. *How did I even love this man as passionately as I did? I don't even know him.* "No. I call the shots. Billionaire, remember? Any proposal or proposition equates to a poor business decision on my end."

Insufferable woman. "Will you at least listen?"

Her expression remained wooden, her posture unchanged.

Feeling desperate, he switched tactics. "Then, I'll go to the press." He regretted the words as soon as he'd uttered them, not really wanting to cause her any stress. Wincing, he waited to hear what she'd say.

Astonished at his willingness to risk everything he'd built, Emmi's arms dropped to her sides. "You wouldn't. You stand more to lose than I do. I'm not saying yes to some manic proposal you've just cooked up, so you can assuage some macho guilt trip. I came to let you know I was pregnant with your child. As a courtesy, I did it in person. Nothing more. Nothing less."

"Emilia, please." Vincenzo dropped from the couch to his knees, begging her now. His hands took hold of hers and his eyes searched for any sign of the past. Seeing her expression soften at last, he cleared his throat, trying to put into words all he wanted to say. "After you left the wedding, Strazzo ran down the aisle and confessed he was in love with my bride."

Emmi gasped.

"It gets better." Vincenzo moved back to the couch, not letting go of her right hand, fearing she'd leave before he could get everything out. "When Sondra refused to listen to him, he told her she was making a colossal mistake by marrying me, citing the most obvious reason—your pregnancy."

"He did what?" she nearly shouted, wondering when Strazzo had developed the backbone to confront Vincenzo. Strazzo had told her firsthand at the coffee shop that he had long been fearful of being on the receiving end of his brother's wrath. Still, she had sworn the little weasel to secrecy, and he'd gone and blabbed it, not only to Vincenzo, but everyone else.

"No worse than what you intended to do," Vincenzo said. "But it doesn't matter. What does matter is whether my single status changes your answer to the proposal?" he asked with trepidation, stumbling over his words.

"What proposal?"

"For god's sake woman, I'm trying to ask you to marry me."

Emilia's gaze flew to his face, scarcely believing the words that issued from his mouth. "Proposal," she said with sudden realization. "I thought you meant proposal… As in, suggestion."

"Do you need time to decide? There's more, if you'll listen."

Her mind racing, she tried to hide the fact that she was now on pins and needles, waiting to hear what else he might surprise her with. "I do suppose I could hear you out, at the very least. What did you have in mind?"

Worried she would slip out of his life as she had at least twice before, he spewed every emotion he'd been holding back. "Strazzo also told me you loved me." He looked directly at her, hoping to see any evidence of love still in her eyes. "It took me over six months, but I finally know, without a doubt, that I feel the same about you. I took a chance, and I hired a justice of the peace and obtained a marriage license… for us to marry. Today." Vincenzo finally released her hand and walked to his desk to pull out a tiny velvet box as Emmi watched him in a dazed stupor. He returned, dropping to one knee, this time in a different context than before. "Miss Emilia, soon to be the mother of my child, will you please put me out of my misery and agree to be my bride? I love you," he said frozen to the spot, hoping he hadn't misread the situation horribly.

Emmi's face contorted with an unreadable expression.

With a hint of humor and his heart in his throat, Vincenzo asked, "Has pregnancy made you hard of hearing?"

"No, I came here to tell you about the baby—" she answered. She had mentally prepared for Vincenzo to be accusatory, thinking her just as foolish as the others before her. But as she looked down on the crown of his head at the little spot where he was going a bit bald, over to his beseeching eyes, which conveyed every one of his emotions, to the fullness of his lips, the length of his lashes, all that she knew and loved about him coalesced. In sickness, health, poverty, or wealth.

She loved him…still.

Closing her eyes, a tear fell down her cheek. "Yes," she said finally, her voice cracking ever so slightly. Her hand shook as he slid the ring upon it. "And yes, I'll marry you now. Whatever you've arranged is fine." Any other woman might have been angry at having been denied a large ceremony. Emmi just wanted the man in front of her for the rest of her life.

Hearing a bump outside the door, Emmi removed her hands from his. "Did you hear that?"

"Oh sure, you can hear perfectly fine now…" he chided Emilia. "Guys," he called out. "She said yes! You can come in now." Vitoria and

Strazzo pushed through the cracked office door, smiling from ear to ear.

"They've been there all this time, haven't they?" Emmi cried, embarrassed they'd had an audience.

"Not only have they been out there the entire time, much of this was Mama's idea. I think if I hadn't done this correctly, she would have come in and proposed to you herself."

"Which parts were your mother's ideas, exactly?" Emmi asked, thinking of the whole awkwardness of the situation and how it smacked more of Vincenzo's doing. He was great at running a company, but not so great at the romance business.

"Oh, when you called and asked to schedule a meeting, Mama suggested you should come here to the house, and then we arranged the finer points of the wedding," he said. "The rest was my idea." He brimmed with pride.

No longer able to hold herself back, Vitoria embraced Emmi in a warm hug. "Congratulations, you two."

Emilia returned her hug, but her face fell as she thought about her business and her billions in the bank. While she trusted Vincenzo, she was also a professional who'd worked hard to get where she was, and she wasn't about to enter a marriage without a prenup.

Vincenzo noticed the question rise in her eyes. "Hang on," he said as he placed a call to Emmi's secretary, whom he now had on speed dial. "Danny?"

"Hello, Vinny Dinny," answered the receptionist rather unprofessionally. Vincenzo had always hated the shortening of his name to Vin, Vinny, or Vinnie. Vincenzo couldn't help but wonder what had gotten into Danny.

"I need the name of the OPV Enterprises lawyer."

"Yes, of course. It's Donald Shear." Danny rambled the number back by rote.

Vincenzo finished penning the number and hung up. He followed up with a call to Donald Shear and asked him to draw up an airtight marriage prenuptial that would go into effect when Emilia married him, and had it sent to his email.

This simple act on Vincenzo's part only confirmed for Emilia that this was the right move, the right man. She looked at him lovingly, letting more of her guard down.

Tutting came from Vincenzo's mother. "Emmi, my dear, please come with me."

"Vincenzo, you should come too. You must see," Vitoria said. "This superstition with the groom seeing the bride in her dress is ridiculous. Benedict and I were dressed for our wedding in the same single-room house of my mother-in-law. We were married forty-two years."

While waiting for the carousel to bring the garment to the front, Vitoria turned to Emmi and invited her to look around in the clothing closet that spanned three levels.

"We're going to talk about these after, Mrs. Eton," Emmi said as she picked a pair of emerald green pumps with a finger, recognizing them from one of her favorite designers.

"Yes, we will have many good conversations, I think," she said, looking down at Emilia's pointed toe and stiletto heeled feet on her bedroom floor. "I have those same shoes in red." She laughed as the motor of the closet organizer brought out an antique full-length bag.

Pulling the garment cases free, Vitoria spoke of the history behind the items. "I have both your father's suit and the dress I wore when I married him," she said to Vincenzo. "They were pressed and waiting for this very moment for over thirty years. If you wish to wear them, please do. If not, I will not be offended. It is simply an offer," Vitoria said with humility and emotion, her eyes cast softly upon them.

Vincenzo reverently took the box with his father's suit in it. He hadn't known his mother had kept it all these years. Excusing himself, he went to go dress in a separate room, his stride purposeful and his thoughts pensive.

"If the gown fits, I would be honored, Mrs. Eton," Emmi said, looking into Vitoria's glistening eyes. The Eton family matriarch had welcomed her into their home and their lives since that first fateful day that she had arrived by mistake. Remembering how she'd thought she was being kidnapped, Emilia chuckled to herself.

Handing Emilia the gown to dress in, Vitoria excused herself to find a suitable necklace and the matching silk gloves to round off the bride's garments while Emilia delicately stepped into the cream silk and delicate lace of the dress. The gown's beauty cupped her in all the right places, hiding the evident curve of her pregnant body, as two tiny pleats shot down the front in a symmetrical line.

Entering the room again, Vitoria lay the items on her bed while she deftly fastened the row of pearl buttons down the back of the gown and pulled on the length of its cape. Rearranging Emilia's luscious curls into a messy bun, she stabbed bejeweled pins in at random. With her hair out of the way, Vitoria picked up the sparkling necklace and draped it around Emilia's neck, gently grazing her collar bone.

Emmi felt a heaviness in her chest as she wished her own mother were here, but a warmth quickly took over her sorrow as she realized that she had gained a second mother. Vitoria gently cupped Emilia's shoulders and turned her around to face her. A mother's love shone through her smile.

"You look exquisite, my dear," Vitoria said, handing her the gloves.

Turning to a full-length mirror, Emilia stared at her reflection for a moment. She was struck by how Vitoria, who didn't know her well, had presented her with such a precious memory of value. It was an antique masterpiece only a seamstress could have sewn. Its intricate lace and beadwork were handcrafted. The dress rightly should have been worn by anyone in her more immediate family, but Emilia felt like an imposter. Addressing her soon-to-be mother-in-law, Emmi cried anew as she spoke these thoughts to Vitoria.

"Honey, it's fitting this dress goes to you. This gown was given to me by my mother-in-law, the same way it is handed down to you today. I'd say it even fits perfectly over the little life you carry within you, just as it did with my son—the man you marry today, my Vincenzo." Emmi's eyes glistened with fresh tears as Vitoria hugged her harder. Vitoria released her and pushed her toward the door. "We have to go. He's waiting for you."

Danny walked Emilia down the aisle and passed her off to the groom.

"Sondra is looking well fed," Vincenzo's great aunt said louder than she realized.

Vitoria's eyes opened in shock and embarrassment. Stifling nervous laughter, she whispered, "That's Emilia, my love. She and Vincenzo are expecting."

"Expecting what?" Janie asked.

"I'll tell you later."

Light laughter went around the nearby guests who'd overheard the whisperings.

Reaching the front of the aisle, Emilia stood next to Vincenzo in the garden under a tiny spray of flowers crawling across a portcullis, mentally writing the words to her vows as the justice of the peace said his part. Her heart thudded with love and disbelief at the sudden turn of events. Vincenzo stared back at her, smiling and unable to look away. Maybe miracles weren't off the table after all.

Emmi reflected on her rather extraordinary life. After the early loss of her mother, Emilia had felt incredibly alone in this world before finding love and companionship with Mason, only to also lose him a few short years later. She thought about how she'd shut off her emotions at that point, fearing anything new would just be taken from her as well. She remembered rising from the ashes of her life, finding a new focus in building her empire from the ground up, and becoming a billionaire. And most recently, she remembered finding herself unmarried and pregnant, the father residing in a land far from her own home.

All Emilia Patric had ever wanted was an ordinary and uneventful life, but it had seemed life had other plans for her. She had grown tired of things constantly changing, having no one to lean on. Perhaps now they were finally taking a turn for the better.

Turning to look at their guests, Emmi saw the many faces of her new family. Countless cousins and aunts and uncles sat on the groom's side, waiting to meet Emmi and congratulate her and Vincenzo on their union. In the front row sat Vitoria, along with Strazzo and Sondra, who were holding hands. *Is that a ring on her finger?* Emmi thought in happy surprise, mentally jotting down some questions for Strazzo.

On the bride's side, Danny had clearly come through for her yet again. Rather than being depressingly vacant, he was among many faces who had gladly come to watch her find happiness for the second time. Soldiers filled the rows, along with faithful employees from OPV Enterprises who had become her friends over the years. She took note of her newest employee, the waitress from the restaurant in Galveston.

Lieutenant Colonel Rodriguez sat stiffly in the front row, a look of stoicism on his face. But Emmi swore she saw the slightest hint of a smile playing at the corner of his lips. On his left sat Gunny and St. Haire, all three in uniform. She inhaled quickly and choked back her tears when she noticed the man in the chair on the lieutenant colonel's right. Chills ran down her arms, imagining the ethereal visage of her late husband staring back at her. Mason's gossamer dream face smiled, his expression full of love and support for her future happiness. She blinked a few times, still locked on him as he blew her a kiss and faded away, his memory fading to reveal an empty chair with a reserved sign draped across the seatback, and a folded flag on the seat.

Stifling a sob, she felt Vincenzo squeeze her hands. "Are you okay?" he whispered, concern crossing his face.

"More okay than I've been in a very long time," she responded, returning his squeeze. It was that moment that she felt the baby kick for the first time. Locked onto Vincenzo's eyes, her own widened and her mouth made an O shape. They both looked down at her bump, imagining their child and who he would become.

"Is Mason happy for us?" Vincenzo asked.

Assuming Vincenzo was referring to her late husband giving his blessing to them, she nodded. "I think he would have been." Looking back up at Vincenzo's face, she realized suddenly that he'd meant the baby. "Mason?" she questioned, a hand on her belly.

"Why not?" Vincenzo countered. "It's the name of a hero, the name of the person who ultimately brought you to me."

Emmi smiled, feeling fulfilled for the first time in many years. "It's perfect."

Her life had turned out nothing like she'd ever expected, but it had all led her to the here and now, to her happily ever after. Ready to make her own version of happiness, she thought about how once in a while, love comes along and creates a perfectly ordinary life.

But only in Texas.

Manufactured by Amazon.ca
Bolton, ON

22959406R00129